NEGATIVE SPACE

A Novel by
MIKE ROBINSON

NEGATIVE SPACE
Enigma of Twilight Falls – Book 2
3rd Edition Copyright © 2021 by Mike Robinson
(Original 1st Edition © 2013 by Mike Robinson)

All rights reserved. No part of this book may be used or reproduced in any manner whatsoever, without written permission, except in the case of brief quotations embedded in articles and reviews. For more information, please contact publisher at Publisher@EvolvedPub.com.

THIRD EDITION SOFTCOVER
ISBN: 1622537653
ISBN-13: 978-1-62253-765-5

Editor: Lane Diamond
Cover Artist: Kabir Shah
Interior Designer: Lane Diamond

EVOLVED PUBLISHING™
www.EvolvedPub.com
Evolved Publishing LLC
Butler, Wisconsin, USA

Negative Space is a work of fiction. All names, characters, places, and incidents are the product of the author's imagination, or are used fictitiously. Any resemblance to actual events or persons, living or dead, is entirely coincidental.

Printed in Book Antiqua font.

BOOKS BY MIKE ROBINSON

ENIGMA OF TWILIGHT FALLS
Book 1: *The Green-Eyed Monster*
Book 2: *Negative Space*
Book 3: *Waking Gods*

~~~

Dreamshores: Monster Island

Skunk Ape Semester

The Atheist

The Prince of Earth

Too Much Dark Matter, Too Little Gray: A Collection of Weird Fiction

~~~

Dishonor Thy Father (with M.J. Richards)

The Talisman Chronicles #3 – Hurakan's Chalice (with Aiden James)

WHAT OTHERS ARE SAYING

THE GREEN-EYED MONSTER:
Editor's Choice at HorrorNovelReviews.com:
"Among the Top 10 Horror Novels of All-Time"

~~~

"Absolutely magnificent."
~ *Shannon McGrew, Nightmarish Conjurings*

~~~

"Literary horror… Every page is full of insight, matched only by the high standard of the writing."
~ *Tom Conrad, The Indie Pendant*

~~~

NEGATIVE SPACE:
"Hauntingly poetic."
~ *Jeff Soyer, Alphecca Review*

~~~

"What a page turner! … Robinson is a fine writer, with an enviable gift for the poetic turn of phrase."
~ *Kitty Burns Florey, author of "Solos" and "The Writing Master"*

~~~

WAKING GODS:
"A disturbing, bizarre and intensely riveting novel."
~ *Leslie Ann Moore, Bestselling Author of "The Griffin's Daughter" Trilogy*

~~~

"Pick it up and don't put it down. Have patience. Enjoy the poetic quality. Consume this book."
~ *Sissy Lu, Book Savvy Reviews*

> "Never does nature say one thing
> and wisdom another."
> ~ *Juvenal, "Satires"*

> "What really interests me is whether or not God had
> any choice in the creation of the universe."
> ~ *Albert Einstein*

> "That I eat and drink is a spectacle for
> the great authors and schools."
> ~ *Walt Whitman*

PROLOGUE

Arondale, California, 1971

"Get *away!*" his mother screamed. "Get away from my house!"

The face stared in from the window, a horrible face slicked by rain and shadowed by night, allowing only glimpses of its distorted features.

Candlelight quivered in the storm-darkened house, causing shadow patterns on the wall to bob, images and sensations for which the potent nightmares of Max Higgins's seven years had ill-prepared him.

"Mom," he uttered.

No answer. His mother Cynthia threw frenetic glances at the window.

"Mom... can you call people?"

Those were his first words in an hour. It felt weird to speak. For much of the storm, he'd been immersed in the drawings now scattered about him.

"Phone is dead," said his mother. "Phone is dead but baby God is here with us and we need no one else."

God is here. God... the face in the window?

No. God comforted. This demon of the watery darkness provided no comfort.

A crack came against the window—spidery, something thrown, followed by a voice.

"Hey!" a man yelled.

"Go away!" his mom yelled back.

In one of the sleet-covered windows a figure emerged, as if sired by the storm itself, and rapped firmly on the glass.

"Max, take my hands."

"Mom—"

"Max, just do what I say. Take my hands."

He obeyed.

"Hey!" the man outside shouted. "We're fucking *dying out here!*"

Things would only get worse. If his mother didn't open the door, the man would surely find some other way in.

"Dearest Lord Jesus," his mother began. "We pray, in this time of fear and desperation, for you to comfort those in need, to guide them...."

As she prayed, his mom closed her eyes, but Max could not. He worried that the darkness might grow hands to strangle him if he took his eyes off the world, or however much of the world was left to see.

The man moved to another window and rapped harder. He banged and shouted.

"...give us your love, oh Lord, and sweep these devil waters and their devil spawn back to the rivers of Hell...."

More banging.

Max clutched the gold cross, hung around his neck for the first time when he was three.

"Bitch, please!"

How many more are out there? Are they bothering other people, like Mrs. Olsen next door? Are we supposed to let them in? Will God be angry if we don't?

'That which you do to the least of my brothers, so you do to me.'

Thunder grumbled, and Max's gaze fell to one of his drawings, one of his many Lone Ranger sketches, then moved up to a crucifix hanging on the far wall, scarcely illuminated by the candlelight.

His mother squeezed his hands. "You remember the story of the Ark, don't you?" she asked. "Noah's Ark, and all the animals?"

Max nodded.

She tried to smile. "This isn't much different. God is washing the world of its sinful creatures."

"Is that what happened to Dad?"

"I don't know, Max, but if the Lord had a good reason for taking him away from us, then we mustn't question it, mustn't give it too much thought."

"Hey!" came again from outside.

The weather continued its assault.

"Mom—"

Suddenly, glass shattered, and Max felt the merciless cold of the storm winds on his face. A window... a window had been broken.

Another one shattered somewhere on the other end of the house.

"Get *out* of here!" Cynthia Higgins shrieked. She turned to Max and started to move away, keeping her eyes on him. "Honey, you stay put, you understand me? Don't move."

"Where are you going?"

She scurried to the kitchen.

Max ignored her request and followed her, watched her shuffle through dark cupboards, listened to the clatter of dishes and pots and pans as prayers dribbled under her breath. Somewhere close, he heard voices, deep and grumbling.

"Max, get over there." His mother frantically pointed behind the counter.

This time, he obeyed. He peeked around the corner, one eye cast toward the shadow-dance in the rest of the house.

His mother sidled up against the wall, beneath the Felix the Cat clock, next to the archway leading into the living room. The frying pan trembled in her hands.

Over the sound of the storm, Max could hear the movement of strangers in the house, toward the dining room.

His mom heard it too, and moved accordingly, huddling over to the kitchen's entryway.

Max watched as a face emerged from the blackness — dirty, wild, unclean. He thought of the stories his mother had told him of lepers, and of demons.

The face smiled, clearly delirious. The figure drifted closer, drawn from the murk.

Shuddering, his mom wrenched from her position and sent the pan straight into the man's primal grin with a metallic *crack*.

A cry rang out, immediately overtaken by thunder. In the white disclosure of lightning, Max saw the man on his knees, a hand clasped over his gushing face, his eyes shut in agony. Blood and drool dripped from his chin.

Max's mother stood over him, her breath heaving, her skin no longer the home of Cynthia Higgins but of something as wild and unclean as the man upon whose head she now unleashed strike after strike. Pummeling.

The pulpy chunks flew and the dark liquid rushed toward the linoleum and Max tried not to think about what it was.

More lightning flashed, and the shadows appeared. More of them had come, a black and tattered battlement.

"Get out of my *house!*" his mom screamed.

He had no idea how many there were, but there couldn't be as many as he first saw. His imagination had exaggerated their numbers.

Yes. That's it.

They closed in.

"Don't worry, girlie," one said. "We'll be gone in the morning."

It all happened so fast, like one of those cartoons where characters move so quickly that they just become blurry blobs.

His mother flailed with the pan but missed.

One of the men's hands caught her wrist, while another took her around the neck. Yet another went for her legs. There was a tearing of fabric as they engulfed her.

She shouted, "Max, baby, get *out* of here please, oh please—"

One of the men lunged toward him, but Max eluded him and tore through the house. He burst from the back door and into the yard, clambered across the lawn and past the fence, onto Clover Street and beyond. The wind and rain sliced into his skin, whipping him as he ran and ran, soaked and directionless.

Eventually, the clouds moved on, like muscle-bound bullies satisfied with a job well done. Max squatted in some mud, surrounded by wet brush, shivering and waiting. He wondered if he was going to die, a concept he'd barely begun to grasp.

If I'm going to die, does that mean I'm going to meet Jesus? Did Jesus create all this? The massive trees, the gross bugs scuttling on my arms and shins?

He didn't want to move. Mom had once told him that if he got lost not to move, because that would only make him more lost. He said nothing, too, as he heard his name bouncing through the woods, issued over rain-darkened pathways. He heard the voices and he heard dogs barking. Somehow, he'd forgotten how to speak, or was too afraid to. Too much *other*-ness haunted this forest, even though, far down in his young mind, it seemed like home.

The voices calling his name drew closer and closer, as did the barking dogs, loud and raucous.

Footsteps. Crunching. Closing.

His teeth chattered, and his lips shook so much, he thought they might squirm away.

Then the brush parted and he saw them: police officers, wearing wet raincoats and drenched hats. The foremost officer smiled, and let out a long exhale.

"Hey there," said the officer, extending his hand. "Got a little wild man here."

PART ONE

"Art, as far as it is able, follows nature, as a pupil
imitates his master. Thus your art must be,
as it were, God's grandchild."
~ *Dante*

Chapter 1

Los Angeles, CA, 1992

Okay, that's interesting, thought Norman Ritter. *A dump with a doorman.*

The aged building squatted on the outskirts of downtown Los Angeles, older than most of its towering neighbors. In the blood-colored bricks and the skeletal creak of the fire escape, one could probably glean some vague history of the whole city, a history so fast and full, stuffed into mere decades.

The man at the door looked homeless, or it was just an act. Ritter had seen plenty of the latter, but usually dwelling coast-side, across the sands of Venice or Santa Monica—the beach-bum-hippie façade, often put on by middle-class white kids.

As he drew closer, though, this man seemed authentic. Shorter than average, he wore a brown trench coat frayed at the shoulders. From the thin shadow of a derby—*right out of old slapstick shorts*—stared eyes sunk in a dwarfish face, a face certainly wise with the dark avenue.

He watched Ritter approach.

"Who are you seeing?" asked the man, holding open the door.

"Um, Max Higgins."

A mucus-clicked laugh. "He's all anyone comes to see here."

"Would make sense." Ritter entered.

The man spoke after him. "Elevator's broken, buddy. Gotta use the stairs."

"Thanks."

Goddammit.

Breath came heavy as he made his way to the fourth floor. A subtle nudge from God, he supposed, to get some exercise. Unfortunately, a broken elevator was bound to be as futile as the numerous hints and articles Angelica had thrust at him.

He reached the door and knocked.

From inside, "Yeah?"

"It's Norman Ritter, Mr. Higgins, from *Direct Canvas*. I'm here for the interview."

"Hold on."

Shuffling inside. Norman adjusted his glasses and clutched his notebook tighter.

The door opened. Save for the packet of hot sauce jutting from his lips like some square plastic raspberry, Higgins looked exactly as Norman had seen him in the occasional photograph. Hair droopy and dark blond, like dry grass. Complexion pale. Blue eyes watery and bloodshot. A long-sleeved flannel shirt hung loosely on his frame, and his jeans were streaked with paint. From his neck dangled a small gold cross.

"Come on in," Max said. "Sorry for the mess."

Norman walked in, stepping over an empty Taco Shack bag. Another bag sat against the wall, full of what appeared to be more hot sauce packets, likely companions to the encrusted plates and utensils swelling the sink. Mousetraps spread about awaited their prey with wooden patience, and in an open closet stood two pillars of old newspapers.

That was the non-art side of the small apartment. The rest of the place was full of palettes, easels, paint rollers, canvases of all sizes, storage for finished or in-progress pieces, paint tubes and canisters of virtually every brand, posed wooden mannequins — anything and everything Norman had ever seen for sale in an art store.

Then there was the wall.

Covered in the yellowed gray ivy of clipped newspaper photos and articles, the wall looked like the work of some tenacious stalker, an unsettling shrine obsessively tended to, a thing uncovered after a terrible crime.

This wall wasn't centered on any single person, though. Rather, it was composed of numerous different people, many of them smiling — reprinted yearbook or family photos. A variety of eyes stared dead and grainy out at Ritter from faces of multiple ethnicities and ages. Other eras, too; one girl's photo was from 1979.

Stringing them all together in one sad theme, a harsh, underscoring word blared:
MISSING

"You collect... missing person photos?" Norman asked. *And there's the insanity*, he thought. *Every artist needs some form of insanity.*

Max nodded. "Those are the faces of my paintings."

"I see," said Ritter, mesmerized by the wall of portraits. "Where did this come from?"

Many, understandably, had noted the faces in Max Higgins' work, the eerie veneer of life in them — the closest in reality a painted visage could get to the haunted-house trope of a portrait's pursuing eyes.

Except, of course, these were not portraits but outlandish surreal pieces, taking cues from Dali, Magritte, with dashes of contemporaries like Kush. These worlds, these mindscapes, spoke to one's fancy while the faces, oddly embossed from the weirdness, spoke to something else.

Max went to his Taco Shack bag and retrieved two more hot sauce packets. He bit down on one and began sucking it like a lollipop.

"Not sure where it came from," Max said. "It just kind of came."

Something lurked behind those words.

"Was there anything that may have inspired it?" Ritter asked.

"My father went missing when I was seven," Max explained, sucking the hot sauce packet dry. "It was always kind of a dark hole in my mind."

"And they never found him?"

Max shook his head. "He went off to work and never came back. Apparently, he never even made it to work that morning."

"Strange. I'm sorry to hear that."

Several blocks over, an ambulance screamed. Ritter jotted notes while keeping an eye on his subject.

Max's gaze wandered from the wall to his scattered artwork, much of it covered in blankets and linen sheets. "I think I wonder about missing people because I've met them. Met them before they disappeared, I mean. Not only my father."

"There were others?"

"Two, actually. One was a girl named Jessica, our figure-drawing model at Rheta Art College. I was in my... let's see... junior year, I think it was. She disappeared during lunch."

The story was darkly humorous to Ritter, and he suppressed a smile. He liked how Max put it: *disappeared during lunch*, in a tone that made the tragedy sound like a natural occurrence.

"Did they ever find her?"

"Yeah, a couple years later. She was all messed up from some brain disorder. A fugue, they said. A kind of amnesia. Creeped me out."

"Who was the other missing person?"

"Hmm?"

"The other missing person. You said there were two others, besides your father."

"Oh." Max wiped hot sauce from the corners of his lips. "The other one was me."

Ritter blinked.

"I was missing for about a week when I was seven, in April 1971, up north. I don't know if you heard about the storm that hit Northern California—"

"Yes, I did. My sister was living up in San Francisco when it hit. Like a monsoon, she said."

"Yeah, it was pretty scary. I think Twilight Falls got the worst of it, but my mom and I were living in Arondale at the time, about fifty miles northeast of there. Storm was still bad, though." Max chewed on the empty hot sauce packet, his expression dazed. "We were waiting out the weather. All power was off, and I... um...." He scratched his head, as if something didn't want to come out. "I ended up getting really scared and just running away."

"Into the storm?"

"Yeah, don't ask me... seven-year-old logic. Maybe I just wanted to face my fear and show myself that it wasn't as bad as it all seemed."

"You could have been killed, though."

"I know. Believe me, I know. But I wasn't. Somehow I ended up in one of the parks on the outskirts of town. I can't even remember all of what happened, but apparently whatever prompted me to do such a crazy-stupid thing is what saved me. The roof of my house caved in."

"Jesus Christ."

"Yeah. My mother was killed. That's why, when they found me, I was sent to an orphanage in San Francisco, until I got a scholarship to go to school down here."

"And you've been here ever since?"

Max nodded.

"How do you choose your... faces... for your artwork? Now that I think back on some of your pieces, I notice you use younger folks more, like your age, or children. Of course, at the time I had no idea they were portraits of real people, but I also suppose that could be why your stuff is sort of haunting."

Max took this in thoughtfully. "I stay away from using the faces that make it on TV. If they're on the news and the entire nation knows about them, then the effect is watered down. I don't even have a TV, actually."

"So you use photos from the newspaper?"

"Many newspapers. I subscribe to ten different newspapers, six from major cities, four from smaller towns. I also come across flyers on telephone poles or streetlights, or bulletin boards. Milk cartons, too. You can find them everywhere, actually... the missing."

"Ironic statement."

Max shrugged.

"You went to school here, right? In Los Angeles?"

"Mm-hmm, Rheta College."

"Would you cite any particular influence in your style? A mentor, maybe? A teacher? Or an artist of yesteryear? I notice your pieces are very much an amalgamation of various styles and influences. Dali, for instance."

Max smacked his lips. "A lot has inspired me—Dali's a given, and many more—but there's something grander for me. My mother used to say that God was the greatest artist. I don't know about greatest, but He's the best one we know, the most prolific. Life inspires life. I'm not just slathering wood or canvas with oil and acrylic, I'm bringing out something in the viewer, a new life, an outgrowth of them." Max paused, threw the hot sauce packet to the floor, and bit open another. "Hard to explain, but that's the hope."

Max lost himself in the wall, then turned toward an unfinished painting of two children traversing a giant spinal cord drawing away toward a setting sun, their hands linked.

"Basically, when someone looks at one of my pieces," Max said, "I like to think that they're starting from a fresh slate, as if they're wiped clean mentally. Everything has been washed away. They're submerged in *my* world, and, one by one, my world will summon back to life the fears, the joys, the loves—everything that we, as a species, came to know and understand—so they can experience it all over. A self-re-creation."

"I see."

"I can give you some salt," Max said. "To take with my words."

"Oh, no, believe me, this is great," Ritter said, jotting more in his notepad. "I'm fascinated by it. I've always been fascinated by your work."

"All right, but the salt offer still stands. I can see in your face you think I'm insane. Of course, with your job, you probably think all artists are insane."

Ritter chuckled. "It's an insanity we need more of."

II

The hot sauce packets weren't doing it. Not tonight. He needed the smoke in his chest, the gentle ashen stroke of the cigarette against his tongue, toxic chemo to drive out this cancerous anxiety. Who knew what exactly was in those hot sauce packets anyway — Max had started to feel they were responsible for his recent indigestion.

At the Taco Shack, he filled up on Mild packets, which were piled free for the taking at the condiments station. He got in and out quickly. Behind the counter, the pockmarked kid had thrown him a wary eye, perhaps getting wise.

Whatever.

Now past midnight, Venice Boulevard lay empty. Streetlights sputtered against the dark, pittances of light against buildings long shadowed, save for one: The Sirens Shop at Venice and Beethoven, aglow in its purple-green squiggles of erotic neon, where for two years now he'd worked the graveyard shift.

Something stirred at the base of a palm tree, and Max jumped, unaware the pile was a live thing. A homeless person, cocooned heavily in sheets and a blue sleeping bag, groaned. As Max passed, he could see the man's wiry hair jutting from the blankets. He walked faster.

He stuck a packet in his mouth and bit it open with one chomp. The spices began their tingling celebration on his tongue. He didn't mind the dark and solitary nature of his work schedule, but he wasn't a huge fan of the transients that emerged during these late hours.

Waiting for him outside the shop were two people, a man and a woman. Never failed; no customers for almost three hours, yet step out for only fifteen minutes and they came pouring in.

"Hey, man," said the guy, long greasy hair bracketing a twitchy face. "Where you been? Me and my girl have been waiting. You guys are twenty-four hours, right?"

"That's right," Max said. "Sorry about that. Was just out for a couple minutes."

The guy placed his arm around the woman's shoulders. She stood expressionless, looking at Max and her twitchy boyfriend with equal indifference, a department store mannequin in a sad glow of skin.

Max tried in vain to ignore the cigarette she was smoking. *That smell.* He wanted to rip it from her lips and shove it between his own.

"You'll have to put that out," he told her, "before coming inside."

The woman never changed her expression, just dropped it and put it out with a black high heel. "You got it, soldier."

Max opened the door and led the couple in. He resumed his seat at the register as they loitered amongst the contraceptives, stocking up on condoms, then drifted toward the shop's impressive selection of adult videos. From the radio droned more discussion of Rodney King—the beating, whether the cops had bludgeoned his rights alongside his bones. Max didn't want to hear it. The grainy video, glimpsed when his co-worker Tyler had been watching it on TV in the backroom, had been enough for him.

Max turned off the radio and took refuge in his sketchbook, sucking more of the hot sauce packet. He flipped open to a sketch he'd been working on, a face drawn from a photo in the *Baltimore Sun*, of a young woman labeled—as so many were—as missing.

The woman appeared to be of late high school or early college age. The photo, Max assumed, had come from her yearbook: sunny grin illuminating her face, a banner of white teeth hung below a sharp nose and two sparkling eyes. They often used yearbook photos for missing teenagers.

He perused the *Sun* article. The girl, Karen Eisenlord, had no history of problems, none they were disclosing, anyway. Apparently, she'd been quite the model student until the last year of high school, when her mother noticed in her an increasing disinterest "in everything."

"She didn't love as much," the mother was quoted as saying. "Then, she just loved nothing."

Max didn't read much more. Normally, he didn't bother reading the articles. He used to, but had stopped once he'd begun selling paintings, as knowing too much about these people tended to taint his vision of them, muddy their clean-slate beginnings on his canvas.

What's that Ritter guy going to write about?
No. Don't think about that.

Max kept sketching, fleshing out the Karen-girl's face from the eyes up. On his drawing pad, she looked to be drowning in white quicksand.

Twitchy man and his stoic girlfriend approached the counter, where he slapped down eight packs of condoms and a cassette entitled *A Spankin' Good Time*.

"All set?" Max asked, rising.

"Indeed, my man."

Max closed his sketchbook and placed it out of sight.

The guy studied him as he rang up the purchases. His girlfriend remained silent.

"I seen you before?" the guy said. "You look familiar."

"I don't know." Max whistled softly, drumming his fingers on the register. "That'll be twenty-two fifty."

The man fished a wallet from one of his cargo pockets.

"What about the beach?" he asked. "You ever been down at the beach?"

"This beach? Venice Beach?"

"Yeah."

Max nodded. Since his Rheta days, he'd sold artwork at the coast, a good place for sales, not just for the *amount* of people but for the *mentality* of the people.

The register coughed up the receipt. Max tore it and handed it over.

"What is that, bro?" the guy asked, peering toward Max's chest.

"What?"

"That."

The guy pointed to the gold cross hanging from Max's neck, and snorted. "You religious?"

"Not really," Max said. "I mean, I don't know, kind of."

"You sure this is the best place to work to please Jesus?"

"I've worn it since I was a kid. Kind of a force of habit, I guess. Feels weird without it."

"All right, bro, whatever floats your boat."

The man took the cassette, glanced at it, then half-turned back toward Max wit a devious look on his face. "Hey, this was made at The Schoolhouse, right? This movie?"

"Yep," Max said. "Pretty much all our movies are made there and sent here."

"It's around here, isn't it?"

"Schoolhouse?"

"Yeah."

The man betrayed a creepy juvenile enthusiasm that turned Max's stomach.

"It's in Los Angeles, yes," Max said. "I couldn't tell you any more specifics. They don't particularly want to advertise themselves... too much."

"I'll bet you know where it is, though, huh? C'mon, you can tell me. It's nothing illegal, right?"

"I'm telling you, I don't have the specific address. Call them. Their number's on the cassette."

"All right, all right." The couple went on their way, the bell chiming with their exit.

The hours didn't talk much after that. Thank God. It was why he'd opted for the graveyard shift. Max loved the solitary, quiet opaqueness of night. He loved even more seeing the watercolor wash of daylight spill upon the celestial canvas, colors frenzied and experimental—the passionate zest of a young artist with new ideas and new designs for the new hours.

At six in the morning, Max Higgins made the hour-long bus journey home and collapsed onto his mattress, where he remained unconscious for the next four hours.

Not long after noon, he crawled from his sleep and flipped open his sketchbook to the drawing of the girl once named Karen Eisenlord.

He had her face—he had *her*—the way he wanted it.

III

Norman Ritter ate at his desk. Lunch had grown far less luxurious in the past two years, whittled down from a wine-complemented hour at a cafe to wolfing crackers over his keyboard. He had to compete, as did *Direct Canvas*. The magazine had increasing company on the shelf. As a result, they'd taken to hiring a slew of younger staff with whom Ritter often felt at odds. He consoled himself that he was in his prime, whatever that might mean.

A colleague named Chris Pemberton approached his desk, carrying a sheet of Xeroxed paper. "Norm, how's it going?"

"Hey, Chris, not bad."

"You're going to have your little bundle soon, right? How's Angie?"

"She's doing fine."

"When's she due again?"

"About a month from now."

"Wow. Get your sleep in while you can."

"Right."

"The Higgins spread looks great, by the way."

"Thanks."

Ritter's profile of Max Higgins, just published, had already begun generating fair buzz. Senior editor Dennis Knowles had decided to feature it prominently on that month's cover.

Pemberton placed the sheet in front of Ritter, an article featuring a black and white photograph of a middle-aged face: creased, deadpan, darkened by the coal-black shadows of the Xerox.

Why do artists never smile? They too cool for that? Too burdened with genius?

"Who is he?" Ritter said.

"Name's Clifford Feldman. He's becoming kind of a thing in the Seattle art scene. Going to have a show just up north in Twilight Falls, at the Peters Museum."

"Feldman?"

"Yep."

"That actually does sound familiar." Ritter skimmed the article, the headline of which read *Top of his Head, Top of his Game*. "He the one that does what he calls 'dream pieces'?"

"Basically. It's more like 'instinct' pieces. According to him, his first major piece was inspired by a dream. Since then he's set out to ignore anything overly conscious when doing his artwork. Says he wants the mindset of an animal when he paints."

"Hmm."

"Apparently, he's stirred a bit of a movement. Calls it Neo-Naturalism."

One piece featured in the article showed a humanoid, several lines beyond a stick figure, running amid charcoal renditions of what looked like wild boars.

"It's like cave art," Ritter said. "Or something."

"Exactly," said Pemberton. "That's sort of the point."

"What's up with this guy? Are you doing a story on him?"

"Well, I was actually wondering if *you'd* be interested. The show up north runs until next week." Pemberton started biting his nails, muffling his voice with his fingers. "I figured since you're good with the offbeat artists, you might like to check it out for us."

"Good with the offbeat artists?" Ritter snorted. "What does that mean?"

"Well, I mean, you covered that guy who put big canvases at the bottoms of buildings or cliffs for people committing suicide to land on—"

"Ted Wilshire, yeah... don't remind me."

"Ted Wilshire, right. You covered him until he was arrested. Now you just came out with this Max Higgins character—"

"He's not too offbeat, actually."

"Really?" Pemberton furrowed his brow. "He paints missing people into his work, right?"

"But the way he approaches it... it's not creepy or morbid. You'd have to see it for yourself. It almost feels like he's trying to find something—an answer, a cure. Not really sure."

"His pieces are strange," Pemberton said. "I don't really know how to classify them. You called them surrealistic in your article, didn't you?"

"No, he doesn't want a label on his stuff. And it's funny—first you think he's surreal, and it is, but then as you see more of it, or look more closely at a single piece, it seems to shift. Very strange. It goes from surreal, to abstract, then maybe hops over to impressionistic. He fills a lot of cracks."

Pemberton nodded. "So what do you think of this Feldman? Knowles was the one who recommended you take a look at it."

"Oh yeah? Not Eric the grad student? Whatever his last name is."

Pemberton snorted. "Where have you been? Eric Fries got fired."

"Huh? When? Why?"

"Something like two days ago. Came into work high as a kite. You didn't hear about that?"

Ritter shook his head as a young woman approached his desk, moving up from behind Pemberton. She wore a large gray sweatshirt, her pants ink-black. The dark attire clashed with her pale skin and blonde, almost fluorescent hair.

Quite young, possibly even a late teenager. Pretty, though.

She addressed Pemberton. "Are you Norman Ritter?"

Pemberton swung a thumb toward Ritter, then moved off with a straight-faced salute.

Ritter studied the woman. "What can I do for you?"

"Sorry to bother—"

"It's okay."

"You wrote that article about Max Higgins, right? The one that just came out?"

"Guilty as charged."

Funny she'd come about the Higgins article, as somehow the girl's demeanor reminded him of the artist. He couldn't pinpoint the similarity, but supposed it had something to do with her anxious eyes, and the cautious way every word climbed her throat.

"What's going on?" he asked.

"I was wondering if you could help me find him."

"Who are you? What's your name?"

"I'm his sister."

"He never said anything about a sister."

"He wouldn't know he had one." She shifted her weight. "Can you tell me if this is his address?"

The girl unfolded a small piece of notepad paper and handed it to him. The handwriting was sloppy, but he could make out most of it.

"No. He lives downtown." Ritter eyed her. "And no offense, but I don't know anything about you. What's your name? Aren't there any other people closer to him that you can go to?"

"No, no," she said, flustered. "Look, I figured you're not going to help me." She fished through her pockets, brought out a business card, and handed it to him. It showed an illustrated silhouette of a curvaceous woman holding a whip, with *The Schoolhouse* written above the address.

The Finest BDSM Club in Los Angeles, it read.

"Give that to him," said the young woman. "He can find me there. Please."

"And you're sure this is the Max Higgins you're looking for?" Ritter said. He held up a copy of his spread. "The artist? The hot sauce sucker?"

The girl looked bewildered, but pointed to Higgins' picture and nodded. "Yes, that's him."

IV

At the moment he thought he heard a knock on his door, Max thought how God had nothing on him, or any artist for that matter. God made life, life that was left to chart its own course once it left His hands. That was the beauty of the divine process. But life made art, and with art, no excuse of elegant imperfection could suffice. Art did not have a universe of time to tumble, explode, burn, run, claw toward perfection. Art had to be perfect as is. Now.

In front of him, now being realized on a 19x24 canvas, appeared the woman from the *Baltimore Sun* he'd sketched the night prior. He'd given her five pages of practice in his sketchbook, swerving clear of the cheery yearbook photo in order to seize a much more poignant face, the way it must have been the moment her life caved in, when she realized she would become nothing but an anxious and despairing memory.

He took the greatest pride in the eyes, because those eyes had shouldered much of the smile in the Karen-girl's photo. In his sketchbook, Max had successfully poisoned those smiling eyes, conveyed in them a kind of existential grief. Hopefully, he would duplicate such success on a larger scale.

As he did with many of his unwitting subjects, Max assumed she was dead. The article was several months old, and he'd skimmed coverage of the investigation. Karen Eisenlord had not been found.

Max rode his own roller coaster as he painted, loving the dizzying heights, the stomach-rolling swirls and falls of color as the winds of his technique brushed the landscape of his imagination. He was high. People like Dr. Farmer, his old therapist, had scientific names and causes for such a sensation, even prescribed pills for it, but to Max it was simply artistic wings caught in a wonderfully strong thermal.

Then came the knock—or so he thought. Max had barely heard the timid knock. His head whipped to the front door, and he listened. Nothing. He applied a few more strokes, then rinsed his brush in the water-bucket.

Another knock. Harder.

Max stopped. "Yeah?"

The voice behind the door said, "It's Norman Ritter, from *Direct Canvas*?"

Max swept a quick eye over his piece-in-progress, then turned the easel to face the wall. No one would see it—not yet.

He went to the door.

Ritter appeared far more casual this time, less officious. He looked mildly confused.

"Hey," Max said. "What's going on?"

"First, I should have asked this before. Who's the guy with the hat, downstairs?"

"Gonzo?"

"The homeless doorman, with the derby."

"Yeah, Gonzo. All the tenants pitch in to pay his salary. Apparently, he used to loiter around the building, so we just put him to work. Come in."

Ritter walked into the studio, nearly stepping on the Taco Shack bag of hot sauce packets. His gaze went back and forth from the floor to Max, who, on his way to the tiny kitchen, stepped over a wad of clothes and bunched-up newspapers.

"You want a drink?" Max said. "Just got some punch and soda. And water. Got bottles in the pantry." He popped open a cola for himself.

"No, no thank you, Max. Did you read the article?"

Max hesitated. "No. I don't relish reading about myself."

'Bullshit.' A stack of eleven issues sat on the bottom of the bookcase. *'Better cover them or Ritter will notice and laugh. Bust you.'*

"I was thinking about our interview," said Ritter. "You mentioned your father's disappearance, your... your mother's death."

"Yeah." Max sipped his drink.

"But you never mentioned a sister."

"Huh?"

"Sister," Ritter said. "You had a sister."

"I never had a sister. What are you talking about?"

"Stepsister?"

"No."

"Niece? Cousin?"

Max shook his head. "My only cousin is named George, and as far as I know he's still a man." A quick beat. "Why? What is this?"

"This girl came to see me the other day. She looked pretty young, and asked about you."

Max shrugged. "I don't know what to tell you."

Ritter looked across the room toward a covered painting.

"How was she asking about me?" Max said.

"Well, for one thing she said she was your sister."

"I told you... no sister."

"Not one you know of, perhaps. Your father *did* disappear, after all. But for all I know, she could be some crazed groupie. I felt it best to at least inform you."

"You think she's crazy?"

"No, she didn't seem like it." Ritter got out the business card she'd given him. "But you never know. She got some bogus address for you, from where I don't know."

"What did she look like?"

There was another knock, a heart palpitation on the door.

Max said, "Wait, hold that thought."

He hurried to the door. One of his neighbors, a man named Renaldo, whose English was a lingual archipelago in a sea of Spanish, stood there.

"Agua all over! Agua all over!" he said. "You talk manager?"

Max nodded rapidly. "Yes, I will."

"El problemo tambien?"

"Uh, no, not a problem."

Renaldo smiled, wide and eager, and the sputtering conversation wound down.

Max closed the door and turned back to Ritter, whose attention had moved to the floor, to his sketchbook. The man was very still.

Max walked over, noticed the writer's surprised expression. "What is it?"

"That's her," Ritter said in a disbelieving breath.

"What do you mean, that's her?"

"This drawing." Ritter pointed at the sketch of the missing Karen Eisenlord from Baltimore. "It's *her*. That's the girl who came to see me."

Chapter 2

I

Max flipped The Schoolhouse business card in his hands, twirling it over and over, constantly glancing at the silhouetted dominatrix, distracting himself from the other bus passengers, the sundown passengers he rarely encountered on his normal bus routes. Sundown faces differed from those of the late-night and early-morning — wearier, more bedraggled.

The Schoolhouse was not far from the Sirens Shop, but he'd never been there, despite their close retail relationship. He'd seen many of their videos, had seen even more covers, yet they'd ceased to do much for him. Had this Karen-girl been featured in any of the videos he'd sold? Had her visage brushed his eyes before opening that issue of the *Baltimore Sun*? Was subconscious familiarity the reason she'd spoken to him from the inky sea of other possible subjects?

As dusk deepened in the sky, Max checked his watch: about five hours before his shift began. He would have time well enough to talk with her. Hopefully she was there; otherwise, he would leave a message. Maybe he could check out the place. It was a new thing, after all, fresh sights and sounds. Inspiration hid in the unknown, unseen, and unheard. Maybe his next Big Work lurked inside its walls. Who knew?

Next? I'd need a first Big Work.
'Tell them you work at Sirens. Get the VIP treatment.'

Behind him, two men quietly discussed the fate of the four officers indicted for assaulting the King fellow. The trial was being moved from L.A. County to Ventura County, where the populace apparently sustained a disproportionate amount of law enforcement officials. One man worried the cops wouldn't see a single prison cell bar.

He approached the quaint Tudor-style house, almost cartoonishly slim. Beams formed sharp angles along the outer walls, its thin windows glaring upon the streets. The house had a tenuous hold on reality. Max took cautious steps up the sidewalk, then noticed someone out of the corner of his eye: a young woman roughly his age.

"This is the place?" she asked Max. "The Schoolhouse?"

"I think so. I've never been here before."

"Me neither," she said. "My girlfriend recommended it to me."

"I'm just here to talk to someone."

They approached the front door in silence. Max was about to knock when the girl homed in on the doorbell and pressed it. From behind the walls and curtained windows, music played audibly. Occasional cries of pleasure rang out, sounding almost theatrical.

An older woman, clad all in black, answered the door. "Hello, welcome," she said, motioning them in. "My name is Rose. Do either of you have an appointment?"

"I have a reservation," said the woman at Max's side, some drill sergeant in her tone. "With Christine for eight o'clock. I know I'm a little early, but I don't mind waiting."

"Perfectly all right." Lady Rose returned to her desk and flipped through two pages of a large scheduling book. "And you, sir?"

"I'm actually not here for a session." He brought out the card. "Is... Penelope here? I'd like to speak with her."

"She's in a half-hour session right now. You can wait if you'd like. She shouldn't be too much longer, although I think she has another appointment at eight."

"That's fine. Just want to clear something up."

With a raised eyebrow, Lady Rose asked, "Are you her boyfriend?"

"No."

"Ah, okay. Sorry. Sometimes we get those around here—jealous significant others."

"You can rest easy."

"Nice to know. You sure you're not interested in a session?" She smiled at him. "What do you do for a living?"

A memory ran through his mind—his co-worker Tyler, sitting with legs propped in the backroom and watching a Schoolhouse video, with moans of ecstatic agony. He recalled the hard fleshy smacks, the grotesque ripples of the woman's buttocks, the red lines across delicate skin, the sloppy look on Tyler's face.

"I'm an artist," Max said. "And I'm not interested, really. Thanks, though."

Rose gave him a knowing smile. "People are afraid of themselves, it seems. They're so worried they're going to be judged when they come in here, but really it's just a release, a liberating break, and it recharges. Puts you in touch with all the things that make us *us* that no one dares look at. You should know about that kinda stuff, being an artist."

Max nodded, half-listening.

A door opened, followed by voices. From one of the hallways, a man emerged — nicely-dressed, blazer draped over one arm, hair gelled, complexion flushed. Pretentiously clean, perhaps he was an investor or banker — someone who played all day in the dollar-cent sandbox.

Maybe his own pretensions as an artist were shining through, but the money-mover types, these Players, these Movers and Shakers, seemed to Max to betray a woodenness of spirit, the cold, mildewed core of anti-enlightenment. They'd reconnected with the savage neutrality of the elements, but at a much... lower level. A deader level.

This man, however, looked revitalized.

"Amazing," said the man. "Simply amazing. I felt so... so comfortable. That Penelope really knows her stuff."

Just seconds behind him came the girl in question, and Max's body stiffened. She wore a skin-tight leather outfit that glistened like oil. A leather cuff hung from her right wrist. She looked vibrant, as well, but an undeniable weariness shaded her expression. Beneath her callused demeanor, Max could still glimpse softness, vulnerability.

It's her! It's her! Christ, it's her!
Karen Eisenlord.

She looked away from her most recent client and saw Max sitting stiff and aloof.

Mr. Mover and Shaker stopped by Rose's desk to set up a future appointment.

"Max," Karen said.

"Are you—"

"Here," she said, grabbing his arm and leading him toward the door. She called back to Rose, "Taking a smoke break."

They stepped out onto the porch. Evening had fallen, bringing the long, steady exhale of the 405 Freeway nearby. Max pulled out a Taco Shack packet, bit into it, and sucked it down fast, setting aflame his mouth, throat, and stomach.

"You're... Karen Eisenlord," he said.

I've been drawing you.

A sillier notion struck him: *I made you live. You crawled out of my sketch, into skin.*

Karen lit a cigarette, which Max tried to ignore as he drained the packet.

"Penelope at work," she said. "But yeah, I go by Karen McAdams now." She blew out smoke. "I thought I might have a visit from you."

"You went to Norman Ritter?"

"The article guy? Yeah." She took in another lungful of smoke and curled it out through her nose.

"Who are you?" Max said.

"I don't fucking know," she said with a smile. "Do you know who *you* are? You have a few years on me so maybe you do."

"Why have you been trying to contact me? How... or... or *why* are you here? You're missing in Baltimore.

Your face is in the paper. By now, everyone probably thinks you're dead."

"I was in the paper?"

Max nodded.

"In Baltimore."

"Yes."

"How do you know that, then? Don't you live here?"

"I subscribe to a lot of newspapers. It's a long story."

"Ah," Karen said. "For your artwork, right? You put missing people in your art or something. I saw it in the article."

"Who are you?"

"I'm your sister. Well, half-sister. My father went missing when I was a kid. Yours did too, right?"

"Well, yeah. What about it?"

"I think we had the same father. What was your father's name?"

"Darren Higgins." Max shook his head as what this girl was saying came crashing into him. "Look, why are you telling me this? I don't talk about my father. I don't talk about my mother, really. And where... where in God's name do you get off claiming to be my sister?"

"Wait here," she said.

She smashed her cigarette against the concrete and went back inside. She returned several seconds later with a creased and beaten photograph and held it out for Max, who plucked it from her fingers.

"Look familiar?" Karen asked, lighting up another cigarette. "I have only one of him."

Max looked at the photo: a gray-haired man in his fifties or sixties, dressed in a long coat and pointing toward the camera, his eyes burning as if prohibiting the photographer from taking the picture. Motion blur smeared the image.

Yes, he does look familiar.

"I don't know," he said. "The picture isn't clear enough, but... I suppose. Why? What does it matter?"

"It matters because of that void he left in your life. The article said he left when you were seven?"

"Yeah."

"I honestly don't know what's worse, knowing your father and having him disappear, or having him disappear before ever getting to know him."

"Why are you saying you're my sister?" Max repeated, his stomach knotting.

"Because I am. I know it. I can't explain how I know, not really. Not yet—" She paused. "But I need you to trust me, and I want to show you some things of mine that I think you'll understand." She let out a stream of smoke. "I ran away from home, Max, and made my way out here. No one knows I'm here, not anyone from that life, at least."

Max had encountered many things in his life far more unbelievable than this Karen's claim, things he had more readily accepted. The idea he had a half-sister seemed entirely probable, especially if there had been no foul play to account for his father's disappearance. Still, this was too hard, not because it was unbelievable, but because it was all too believable. All too possible.

He finished the hot sauce packet and fished out another one.

"Oral fixation's done a number on you, huh?" Karen said. "Let me guess—fellow ex-smoker?"

He nodded. No one had ever understood that before, not without first going through a puzzled face.

"How long did it take you to quit?"

"Like twelve tries," Max said.

"Not too bad. I'm into double digits for sure. Like Mark Twain said, it's easy to quit smoking. I've done it hundreds of times."

The quote elicited a short-lived smile. Behind them, the front door opened and Karen's Mr. Mover and Shaker came bustling out of the house. He regarded Karen and beamed. When he spied Max, his giddy spark died.

"Thanks again, so much," he said to her, backing his way down the front walkway. He tried to put on his blazer but had trouble with the right sleeve. He laughed to cover up his embarrassed grunts.

"Anytime," Karen said in an exaggerated Southern twang. Penelope's voice, Max guessed. "Come back real soon, hun."

Her dainty fingers waved in the dark, almost musical, like they should be accompanied by chimes.

Mover and Shaker's heel struck a sprinkler and he stumbled, chuckled, then turned around and continued toward a Jaguar parked under a streetlight.

"Your client looks flustered," Max said.

"That's James. That was only his second session here, actually. First time was a little hard getting him to do anything, he was so terrified that he was doing something wrong or immoral or against the law. I told him to relax—we all told him to relax—but he was petrified. Said he didn't want to cheat on his girlfriend."

"Doesn't seem like cheating."

"Right. No one's having sex here. It's just a healthy way to unleash your fantasies, your natural human curiosities."

"So he's pretty broken in by now, I take it?"

"Eh, kinda. He's still having trouble, probably feels embarrassed. But whatever, I know he loves it. I can see it in his face."

She fell into a prickly silence.

Despite the age difference, Max felt a fast-growing affinity with Karen. They'd been dwelling on the same floor their whole lives, but had just now met in a random sprint for the elevator that would either take them high, or plunge them farther down into places they'd been to before, and to which they never wanted to return.

"Hey, I get off pretty soon," she said, flicking the cigarette onto the pavement. "Would you like to see where I live? I want to show you something, too."

"I start work in a couple hours." He felt lightheaded. "So we'd have to make it fast. Depending on where you live, I suppose."

"I don't live far, just over near Santa Monica." She checked her watch. "Listen, I'm due for another client pretty soon. It's a half-hour session so it shouldn't take long, but I've got to get ready."

"Okay."

"Can you wait for me?"

"I think I can manage."

Karen gave a bittersweet smile and went to change or spruce up the room or do whatever needed to be done.

Max followed her inside, took a seat, and made small talk with Lady Rose. He found a broken pencil in his pocket and amused himself by sketching on the back of forgotten business cards in his wallet, until Lady Rose noticed and offered him a wad of printer paper. He sketched the interior of the house, Lady Rose herself, and anything else that caught his eye, until

Karen came out as Karen, undressed of Penelope, and announced she was ready to go.

II

From inside the dark room came sputtering gasps and breaths of someone either in dire pain or pure ecstasy. Karen flipped on the lights, revealing in all its unkempt glory the apartment and its current occupants: a young man and woman in a ball of sexual embrace on the couch.

Much of their bodies remained clothed, but when Max saw the white loaves of the man's ass, he averted his gaze.

Karen stood in the room, hands on her hips, watching them.

"Hey, K," the woman said between breaths, muffled by the man's shoulder.

Karen sighed. "Viv, did you get more milk like I asked you to?"

"They were out of one-percent, so I got two. Hope it's—" *Gasp.* "—okay."

Karen went to the fridge and pulled it open as gratified moaning filled the air.

"Onepercent?" Karen barked. "I told you to get soy milk!"

"Oops... Oh God yes, yes, *yes*, oh oh oh *right there*—"

Karen shut the fridge door and motioned for Max to follow her into her bedroom.

He did so with alacrity, and whispered, "They're having *sex*."

"Fuckin' idiot," Karen hissed. "Can't remember a single fuckin' thing I fuckin' tell her." She picked up two bras and a pair of panties and tossed them into a bulging hamper.

"What the hell's going on?" Max asked. "Who are they? Your roommates?"

"Vivian's my roommate. That's her boyfriend, or at least this week's."

"Does she always just do it right out where anyone could walk in?"

"Pretty much."

"And the guys don't care?"

"Nah, they get used to it, with the amount of times she goes at it." Karen shook her head. "I think she burns through a whole marriage's worth of sex in like two weeks."

Karen threw aside more clothes and books, some of which—such as Nietzsche's *Twilight of the Idols*—looked old and beaten. At the end of her search, she lifted something heavy: a photo album.

No family photos appeared inside, however—no trips, no boyfriends, couples, or birthdays. No candid moments. Instead, it contained page after page of aged newspaper cutouts, and a swarm of the same word that held ominous reign over Max's studio wall.

Missing.

"I collect them too," she said.

Words amassed in Max's head, but lost their identity. He had no idea what to say.

"I'm not as artistic as you," she said. "But I think we do it for the same reasons."

"We do?"

"Sure. Because of *him*. If we look into the world of the missing, maybe we'll catch a glimpse of him. If we scour articles, publications, flyers, anything, we might stumble upon something. Maybe your artwork is like glorified *Have You Seen Me?* flyers you hang in galleries and in people's homes. You want these people found. You want him found."

"But why do you keep a book full of strangers?" he asked.

"Same reason, I guess, as you do: to give them a home."

He didn't say anything.

"Thing is, I think he's done this a lot," Karen continued. "I think he starts families all over the country, maybe even all over the world, and runs. Maybe I'm just hoping to snag the next report of a missing father or husband, and bingo, catch him in the act."

"So, if that's the case," Max said, "you've probably got tons of brothers out there, and, maybe, I have a lot of sisters. Why come to me?"

"Well, for one thing, I think it was your family he left when he started mine."

"Excuse me?"

"He left when you were... what... seven? In 1970?"

"Yeah, around then."

"I was born in 1973."

"Look, I don't know what to tell you," Max said. "I'm sorry. I don't have much more info than you do, and there's no proof at all that we had the same father."

She held his gaze. "You probably don't have any more info than I do, because I have these."

She pulled out a drawer full of folders and loose papers, riffled through them, and unearthed a clipped-together stack of papers, which she handed to Max. They were drawings. On seeing the first one—a cowboy on a horse, rendered in child-like crayon—his eyes widened.

"I did this," he said. "It was one of my Lone Ranger drawings."

He flipped through them all. Some were drawings of friendly-looking monsters, some of Biblical scenes, some of dinosaurs, many of cowboys. Karen had about ten of his childhood drawings. Scrawled proudly on the back of each one, in his mother's handwriting, was his name, age, and the date.

"I haven't seen these in over twenty years," he said. "How did you get them?"

"They were part of my father's stash, I guess." She shook her head. "Honestly, I'm not sure. According to my mom, he would get occasional letters from California. She once got suspicious and opened one of them, and it was one of your drawings."

Chills ripped through Max's bones, and his hands grew clammy. He'd produced hundreds of drawings in his childhood, ever since his four-year-old hand first picked up a crayon with serious intent, yet throughout the blaze of creativity, he'd never kept track of his stuff. It was very possible that, unbeknownst to him, his mother could have snuck some away.

But she didn't know what happened to Dad, either. She had no idea. She claimed he must have done something, that God must have plucked him from our lives because –

'*– because –* '

"Your mom," Karen said. "Was she very religious?"

'*– baby God is here with us and we need no one else –* '

Max nodded. "Why?"

"Mine was too. Pentecostal. From the moment I could speak, I couldn't stand it. Weird, huh? I don't know what it was. I had an inborn aversion to it. My mom denied I did, and I denied I did. I went along with the rigmarole, though, until I just... couldn't stand it any longer. I remember being scared and hating God for what he'd do to her at church. It freaked me out how she would break down in tears, mumble, and speak in tongues. I was terrified. It was like a psychosis, I swear."

Max remained quiet.

"I'm sorry about what happened to your mom, by the way," she said. "I don't think any kid, or anyone, should have to go through that, seeing their whole house, their whole world, collapse like that."

"The house didn't collapse," Max said. "That's just what I told Mr. Ritter. My mother was murdered by a small band of vagrants that wanted shelter from the storm. I barely escaped."

"Oh my God...." After a slow, digesting pause, she said, "You know I didn't expect you to fill in any more holes, Max. On our father, I mean. But finding each other is at least something, a step we can share. So I guess it does kind of fill in something."

"You still haven't answered—"

"What I'm sort of jealous of," Karen said. "Well, I don't know if I'm jealous, really, but...."

"What?"

"It's just... you got him for seven years. I had him for only three. I'm wondering why he stayed the four extra years with you."

"Don't ask me. Honestly, we really weren't that close. Only time he would pay attention to me was when Mom said something or...." He gestured toward the first red-crayon sketch of the Lone Ranger. "Or when I would draw."

"Oh."

"Yeah, that's one thing he did. He encouraged me to draw, to be creative. I suppose, when you consider what I ended up doing, he's had a pretty big influence, but it wasn't really him that made me want to draw. The crayons and pencils and markers were all little escape pods for me. I guess Dad helped me with that."

"We didn't have a dad, Max, not really," Karen said. "We had a father."

For a few seconds, the only noises came from Vivian and her catch-of-the-week reaching new orgasmic heights just beyond the wall.

"Why would my mother send my drawings to you?"

"Wasn't to me. It was to him. As you just said, he was most interested in your drawings. Maybe he wanted to see how you were growing, progressing. Don't fucking know."

Not wanting to add to Karen's fire, Max just said, "What was your father's name?"

"Robert Eisenlord. That's what he said, anyway." She studied Max. "Did you ever paint him?"

He reached into his back pocket, dug out his wallet, opened it up, and let dangle an accordion string of business card-sized prints of his artwork.

"You keep tiny copies of all your pieces in your wallet? That's amusing."

"Why?"

"Most people keep pictures of boyfriends or family in there."

"Well, what family is there to put in here?" Max said. "And I don't have a boyfriend."

"Heh, sure. So... what's your favorite?"

"I don't know. Am I supposed to have a favorite?"

Karen stood silent.

Max scanned the column of pictures and pointed to one. "There's him, the one with the sort of alien landscape and the moons. I called it *Moon Watch*. It's one of the few paintings I've just left in my closet."

"Never sold it?"

"No, never tried."

"Why him in this piece? Any reason?"

"Honestly don't know. I'd lost his picture and couldn't find it for years. I almost forgot about it, actually, but when I started this piece, I didn't have any faces that inspired me, none that just, you know, punched me." Max stared at the thumbnail. "Then... I'm sifting through this pile of stuff... I don't even remember what... probably a bunch of magazines and newspapers.... Anyway, it's just there, this photo I haven't seen in God-knows-how-many years, staring at me, like a mathematician finding that one key answer."

"You like to do fantasy, huh?"

"That's the real art to me: bringing out the things in the cracks, the weird glue holding us and the world together."

Karen snorted. "Makes sense. He looks younger than my photo, by the way."

Max shrugged, then collected the accordion string of photos and squished them back into his wallet. "I'm paranoid about something happening to them. That's why I keep a record in my pocket. I always think someone's going to break into my place or set it on fire or something. So if that happens, I'll at least have some proof that all my stuff existed."

Karen asked, "What if someone mugs you?"

"I got back-ups," he said matter-of-factly, even though he didn't.

"You look like you could use a drink," she said. "Same here. We got Gray Goose, Crème de Menthe, and I think Viv's guy might have brought over some beer—"

"I've got work in like an hour," Max said, checking his watch. "And I don't drink."

"Well I do. Follow me."

III

James Cannon pulled into the driveway, shut off the engine, and sat in darkness. The kitchen light was on. *Dammit.* Teresa always seemed to be here. She was in there for sure, milling about, washing things, cooking, being a girlfriend, warm-up as a wife. *No.*

Penelope, what would it be like to fuck you?

The ticking of the cooling engine beat in rhythm with his pulse. He didn't want to get out of the car. He didn't want to have to put on a smile and hug and kiss Teresa and relate to her all the shit from the firm, like the client with thinly-veiled ties to the *Family* that he was arguing should *not* go to jail. Teresa made the food and would expect him—some pathetic pot-luck fashion—to bring conversation to the table.

Minutes rushed into oblivion, and James sat still. The engine had stopped, leaving behind the lonely dull throb of his pulse. Outside, crickets chirped their tinny chants. He thought about his exes. How good had they been? Had he even really chosen them? Like Teresa, they seemed more to happen *to* him, stumble into his lap as dubious natural phenomena.

He picked up the car phone, keeping watch on the window, and dialed his home number. He could hear the phone ring inside and saw Teresa's shadowy form move from the sink to pick it up.

"Hello?" she said.

"I thought we weren't going to pick up the phone at my house."

"Oh! Hi, James. I'm sorry. I just thought it might be you. I was going to call you anyway to make sure about dinner. You're coming home now, right?"

"Check the driveway, Babes."

The shadowy form came back into view over the kitchen sink and waved at him.

James grinned.

"Come on in already. Dinner's waiting."

"Oh."

"You got my message this morning, didn't you?" she said. "You didn't already eat somewhere, did you?"

"No, no, don't worry. My stomach's growling. I'm coming in."

"Great!"

"Oh, and Teresa Babe?"

"Yeah?"

"Don't pick up the phone when I'm not around."

He hung up.

An exquisite feast awaited him: pot roast, mashed potatoes, macaroni salad, asparagus—all filling his stomach through his eyes.

"Wow," James said. "This is certainly nice. Thank you."

"Of course! It's a bit of a celebration. You were able to come home at a decent hour."

We're celebrating that now. Jesus. Everything's a celebration. Why not make every day a holiday, stop kidding ourselves with our fucking excuses and fill up and ride the days away detached and intoxicated? World can't touch us then. No. Can't touch us.

"I know," he said. "It's been a little bonkers."

Changes were afoot at the firm, bringing higher profile cases and throwing him into redeye hours. Of course, it had its upsides: namely, a built-in excuse when he wanted to grab beers with Joe or Larry, or snag a bag of Mickey D's, or... or....

The Schoolhouse. Yes, the fucking Schoolhouse.

She knows, doesn't she? Everybody knows. Somehow, word will get back.

He gave his hands a quick rinse under the faucet, then sat at the table.

"This looks great, Babes," he said, colorlessly. "Thanks again. Wow."

"The macaroni dish over there is actually a recipe I got from Barbara. Her mother made it for Susie's shower and it was excellent. I hope I got it at least half-right."

"I'm sure it's fine."

They sat across from one another and began serving themselves, scooping and piling the food onto the china. They sat and ate, James shoveling items into his mouth and happy for the quietness.

Teresa fidgeted. "They keep showing that awful Rodney King beating on the news," she said. "Man on CNN said it's become television wallpaper."

"That's a good way to put it. It sort of has."

"I know. I think it's disgusting. I'm sure those cops will get theirs." She took a drink of water. "How'd everything go today?"

"He's not exactly a model scout himself, that King fellow," said James. "He's an ex-con. Robbed a convenience store, I think. And I hear he was on PCP when they pulled him over."

"I don't know about that. All I saw was a helpless man pummeled by a ton of cops."

"Bad timing to turn on the video camera, is all I can say."

"I just wish they'd stop showing it. Everyone talks about how horrible it is, but they keep playing the thing over and over."

"Do you watch it when they do?"

"Hmm?"

"Do you watch the video when they play it?"

"No, I turn it off, or switch channels."

The tinkling of glass and porcelain accompanied the chime of the kitchen clock, and James shifted in his chair.

"So how was everything today?" Teresa asked again.

"All right. Firm got a new client who's suing PharmAids drugstore for kicking her out for breastfeeding. Larry's representing."

"I see. Well, I hope he does all he can. If men can jog almost naked in Speedos, I don't see why women can't breastfeed."

"Oh, also, I don't think I'll be able to make it to Helen's party tomorrow."

"What?"

"I've got the closing for the Bendoni trial this week, and...." James waved his hands in the air, hoping the gesture would adequately speak *too busy*. "It's going to be madness. I'll be wiped out. I already am. Maybe sometime this weekend we can make up for it."

Teresa threw her fork onto the plate, sighed, and sat back in her chair.

"What?"

"It's not just me, James," she said. "I hope you realize that. I'm not being selfish here and just thinking about me or our relationship and how all your work is affecting me. I'm also thinking about you."

"What about me? This is my job—"

"Yes, but it seems to be sucking the life out of you. Talking to you lately... it's almost like talking to a computer."

"I haven't noticed anything."

"Of course you haven't." Teresa calmed and tried to smile. "You've got your life sucked out of you, remember?" Her words wore thin dark garments of humor.

James grunted.

"Just look at yourself, James, that's all I'm asking. Self-reflect once in a while. Are you fulfilled, or just distracting yourself? You haven't sold a sculpture in ages...."

"I've sold two sculptures in my life and you know it. It was something I did as a hobby, that's all. It was never a lifeline for me. Plus, I don't think I was ever very good."

"I thought you sold more than two."

"Nope."

"Okay." Teresa sighed. "It was never a lifeline, but it was something different. It was a playground for you. It gave you such energy and enthusiasm. I just miss that."

"I was never sure about myself as an artist," he said. "Never had many original ideas."

"What about the gallery? You and my father always loved talking about it, but it never happened. Now that he's leaving me the trust—"

"I can still do that. I still want to. Just a matter of finding the right time."

"That's not the only real reason you're keeping me around, is it, James?" Teresa said, clearly joking.

"What?"

"The trust. Dad's trust."

"Shut up," he said, lightly. "You know I also keep you around for the food. Now where's my cake, woman?"

She smiled a tight-lipped smile and they continued eating in scattered silence.

After dinner, Teresa busied with the dishes.

James wandered upstairs to the bedroom and went to the closet, where under his clothes he found the relics of himself—his sculptures. First realistic, which, if he were honest with himself, were lame attempts, then more a flavorful foray into abstraction. Late high school and early college—and the long, daunting summer in between—had been the most creative stretch of his life.

His "art affair," as he called it, had earned its name for its secrecy. Pops the Judge was never one for the arts, muttering of their uselessness. Thus, it was for James a hidden passion, surfacing only in bouts of inspired free time, respite from hours of study or exams. Way back in the day, in grade school and part of junior high, James had been The Campus Artist, the one solicited by peers to draw new dragons, superheroes, or scantily-clad women.

Then he'd done that one of Pam Gardner naked, being devoured by dogs. That one had done it. *Oh man. Teacher. Principal. Mom. Pops the Judge. A cold solar system of eyes.*

Unbeknownst to his father, James had applied to two art schools, one of them the locally renowned Rheta Art College. He'd been turned down by both, which brought relief and dejection.

"Hey you."

James turned to Teresa, and flashed a sullen half-grin. "Hey," he said. "I'm just going through my old stuff in here."

"I can see that."

"What are you doing?"

"I'm getting ready for bed, that's what I'm doing." She began to disrobe. "Kind of a long day. Are you going to join me?"

"No, I still have work." He placed the lid back on one of the boxes of artwork, then flicked off the closet light and stood in the doorway. "I think I need to wrap up some work for tomorrow's closing. Did you call your dad?"

"Yeah, he's hanging in there." Teresa sighed. "He's still coherent, of course. Asked about you, how you're coming with the case."

"That's good."

"How is it coming, by the way?"

"Who knows, by this point? I'm defending every Italian-American stereotype rolled into one." He rubbed his eyes. "If I don't get him off, the *Family* will probably come over, pump me full of lead."

"Don't say stuff like that," Teresa said. "Please."

He headed to the door. "I'll be downstairs."

After tinkering with his closing argument, James sat on the couch as the television flickered across the darkness.

Fucking late-night TV. The news programs, jawing about the same story, the story that was constant across every station. The Rodney King Wallpaper. Endless reminder of the African savannah from which we came.

'Jesus, listen to yourself.'

Again, they played the video, offering more layers of commentary, diluting the word *expert* because there were so many said experts adding their two cents: psychologists, sociologists, criminal justice people, lawyers like him.

King thrashed in the center of a ring of cops raining furious blows upon him, their limbs strikes of lightning upon his crippled, trembling body. Officers swarmed around him, scooting into better places to send their attacks.

James moved on.

The Spice Channel was nothing new — butts and breasts and lathering. Stale. He turned off the television, sat back, and fell into a late-night daydream informed heavily from his recent session at The Schoolhouse. Was it open this late? Maybe he could stop by. But Penelope probably wouldn't still be there. Besides, he couldn't overdo it. He cashed hefty checks but that shit was expensive. Not only that, the thing itself was best spaced out. He didn't want his sessions with Penelope to grow stale, though right now such a prospect felt impossible.

And if it does, there are always other girls.

He fell asleep on the couch.

IV

For the immersive and peerless entertainment, if nothing else, Max often made the lengthy bus trip to Venice Beach, even without pieces to sell. He'd also made himself a promise that no matter the heights he might achieve as an artist, no matter the fame that might befall him, he would always craft works to be sold specifically *here*. He had started at the beach and, when he could, he'd always return.

He carried five pieces under his arm, all 9x12 canvases varying greatly in age: one of them, a piece called *Geometric Skull*, had been in his closet since his senior year at Rheta. Another, far more intricate piece titled *Angel Grass*, had only three weeks ago seen its last brushstroke.

Sandwiched among them, as it had been for the past ten years, was *Moon Watch*, the one bearing the likeness of his father. He'd never put it up for display, but maybe that would change. Talking to Karen Eisenlord — or Adams, or McAdams, or whatever name she had now — had shaken his feelings toward the piece, and he wasn't sure in what way; like snow in a snowglobe, they would have to settle before offering any clarity.

A homeless man rested on a nearby bench, his torso propping up a cardboard sign. He jingled a cup of loose change. "Support your local wino!" he shouted. "Help me to a liquor store!"

Max went to his usual spot and set up shop, and noticed that several yards over, another artist appeared to be watching him. He was kind of stocky, bearded, with grungy hair jutting below an old ball cap — a giant lawn gnome regrettably granted modern life.

Max noticed a greater variety of media in the man's offerings than his own: homemade blankets, woven baskets, sculptures, and oil canvases. *Outdoing me*, Max thought. *Maybe I should move.*

Then the man approached him, casual, hands in the pockets of his denim jacket. "Interesting stuff there. My kinda shit."

"Thanks," Max said. "Some of them are pretty old, but figured I'd flush them from storage."

"I hear you." He held out his hand. "Dwayne."

"Max." They shook.

After minor hesitation, Dwayne pointed to *Moon Watch*. "Looks like Germain there."

"Germain?" Max said, blood running faster in his veins. "Who's Germain?"

"The legend of Count Saint Germain. You know it?"

"No." Impatient, impatient.

"He was a fellow from the eighteenth century, alchemist, jack of all trades, still alive, supposedly — achieved immortality through all his tinkering. Of course, all kinds of crazies abuse this story, saying they're the new Count and whatnot. That face in your piece there just reminded me of the latest."

"What do you mean? How'd you hear about all this?"

"I'm obsessed with all that mysterious unexplained stuff, that's how. Got all those books, saved every article I could find. And you let me know if you missed any *Twilight Zone* episodes, cuz I got 'em all on tape, every goddamn season."

"This is actually a portrait of my father," Max said. "Or, at least who I thought was my father."

Dwayne's lips tried for a smile but fell short as he clearly recognized Max's discomfort. "Your father?"

"Yes."

"I could easily be mistaken, Maximo, you know that. Don't mean to insinuate that your dad is a crazy claiming to be a three-hundred-year-old count."

Max said nothing. He also marveled silently at the man's nickname for him. *'Maximo.'* Who knew where that came from, but it had come quick.

Overhead, the sun struggled to crack the marine layer as people swarmed and bustled, the usual endless school of tattooed, skateboarding, dog-walking fish.

"If you don't mind my asking," said Dwayne. "What happened to your pop?"

"Disappeared."

"Foul play?"

"Don't know. Never knew if it was purposeful. He just... *poof*. Haven't seen him since I was seven. He's like a dream."

"Sorry to hear."

"Looks like something's biting," Max said, pointing toward Dwayne's camp.

An attractive couple, hands linked, snooped about the pottery section. The woman picked up a bowl with designs that looked almost hieroglyphic.

Dwayne rushed over to meet them, and Max relieved his lungs of a long-held breath.

Germain. Count Germain. What in God's name is all this?

He took *Moon Watch* from public display and propped it against a nearby trash can. For now, he would hold on to it.

The man named Dwayne was apparently a good salesman, as the couple walked off with the bowl and rejoined the flowing channel of people. The woman held the artifact, but the guy had dropped the cash for it.

Come the inevitable split, which one would it go to?

Dwayne returned with hands jammed into his faded Levi's.

"Congrats," Max said. "What was that you sold?"

"A bowl."

"No, I mean—"

Dwayne chuckled. "I know what you mean. It's a fertility bowl, based off old South American tribal myths that a man fills it with hot water and soaks his penis for a while if he's impotent. S'posed to Popeye you right back up."

Max looked at him blankly.

"I think I've seen you and your stuff," Dwayne said. "You look familiar. Did you have a show or anything 'round here?"

"Last show I had was at the Art Institute on Ocean Park. That was a little while ago. I sometimes come here to sell stuff."

"No, I don't think I've seen you here. Oh! The magazine...." Dwayne snapped his fingers to the beat of his thoughts, trying to recall something. "Direct... Direct...."

"Direct Canvas."

"That's it!"

"Yeah, they had a spread about me in the last issue."

"Right, right. You use... what... ah... missing persons or something in your art? There was some kind of funny little twist about it."

"Well, you got it."

"Right. And yeah, your father went missing and everything, too. I gotcha, I gotcha."

A stale pause ensued.

Please leave. But no.

'You don't want him to leave. You want to talk to someone. You want company. Besides....'

"So why are you obsessed?" Max said. "With, you know, weird things?"

"With Forteana?

"What?"

"Forteana: umbrella for everything weird—ghosts, aliens, Bigfoot... you name it. Charles Fort, my dear. The bedrock of my life. If you want, I can show you. It's all in my van. Call it my little mobile cave of inspiration."

"Little cave of inspiration?"

"Mobile cave, yeah. My van. I drive it all over the place. I hunt up reports of things like Bigfoot and all his lesser known cousins and siblings and friends, and check 'em out for myself. It's a living. Well, not really, but it's my kinda living."

"Are you going to publish a book or something?"

Dwayne shrugged. "I just take it one step at a time, Maximo, one step at a time."

"Why do you do it then? For kicks?"

Dwayne shrugged again. "I suppose so. Someone has to look into all that. Most brush it off, shove it into corners." He coughed, violently, then continued in a thin voice. "It's fine, though—just gives people like us more room to explore those corners, right?"

"I guess."

"I'm not gonna stick around for much longer," said Dwayne. "How long you clockin' in here for?"

"I don't know. However long I feel like. I took the bus here from downtown, so I'm probably going to stay awhile."

Dwayne winced. "Downtown. Yowzers. Well, I can give you a tour of the cave and show you this Feldman guy, if you're interested. Won't take very long."

"Feldman?"

"Yeah, Clifford Feldman... he's the guy claiming to be Count Germain." Dwayne pointed broadly toward Max's collection of canvases. "He's an artist up north and I got info on him. See if he rings a bell."

"Um, I don't—"

"I know you got your stuff out here," Dwayne said, "But we got it covered. Hey, Johnny!"

Max followed Dwayne's eyes through the crowds. The face reacting to *Johnny* was the vocally honest man jiggling a cup for liquor money.

"Yo Dwayne!" Johnny said. "What's up?"

"You watch our stuff here?"

Johnny staggered over. "Sure thing."

Dwayne offered him a two-fingered salute and, with the deftness of a Vegas dealer, shuffled off five ones into the man's palm.

Max hesitated, unsure.

"C'mon, Maximo, we'll be back in a jiffy."

As he placed a friendly hand on Max's shoulder, Max had a faint, tingling notion that Dwayne already knew him, and knew him well.

An explosion of newspapers in here — of magazines, of computer printouts — a contained burst of media plastered across every available surface in this wide-bodied vehicle. Max took it all in, amazed for reasons both complimentary and insulting to Dwayne. A small TV and VCR sat tucked in the corner, fortified by a wall of VHS tapes.

As disorganized as it initially seemed, each... "phenomenon" did, in fact, claim its own region in the van. The Bigfoot and Yetis and other terrestrial creatures lurked in the area of the left back-window, surrounded by foliage of blurry photos, artwork, and children's drawings of other, even more bizarre creatures Max had never heard of before. The space around Dwayne's makeshift bed was a shrine to lake and sea monsters. Perhaps appropriately, UFOs and "sky things" occupied the ceiling, stretching from the rearview mirror to the back windows.

"Yep, this be my humble abode," Dwayne said, crawling inside. He plunked himself on the bed. "It's always on the move."

"You live in here?"

"Sure do. It's my home and my office and my car all at once. Not to mention my studio. Even with all the technology rolling out nowadays, I'm sure you'd be hard-pressed to find a better system than that."

Max remained just outside the van, between the back doors, trying to absorb it all but finding too much to absorb. He wondered if Ritter or others had felt this way when seeing his wall.

He noticed a gun in a duct-taped holster, just below the driver's seat. Max didn't say anything about it, only continued looking until his gaze settled on a tantalizing exhibit of scantily-clad women, photos raunchy enough for the Sirens Shop.

"We can't all have just one drive," Dwayne said. "I got a lot of time to myself."

"Touché."

Dwayne affectionately slapped the ceiling, accidentally peeling loose an article which he smoothed back into position. "Got this baby in the late seventies," he said. "Still runs like a dream. I pay good attention to her, and as long as I keep selling my art, she'll be gettin' me to where I wanna go."

"Where do you go?" Max said, picking up a random scrap of newspaper with the headline: *Legendary Chupacabra Strikes Texas Town?*

"Anywhere I haven't been, basically. If I hear or read about something that piques my interest, I might check it out, but I've actually been in L.A. for longer than expected. Haven't sold as much as I've wanted."

"Where do you keep all your artwork?"

"Public storage, mostly, but I keep my supplies with me in here, in case I'm in The Muse's sniper-scope and somethin' strikes me. Never know."

"Where's the picture of that Feldman guy you were telling me about?"

"Oh yeah. Look over by the passenger's seat." Dwayne craned his neck around, shifting his body weight so Max could see.

Torn-out pages and Xeroxed articles covered a portion of the window, many complemented by photos. Edging closer, he noticed one consistent phrase across the literature: Twilight Falls.

"It's got its own section," Dwayne said. "There's something about that town you can't touch. In fact, it's the only sort of... hmm... *elusive* thing I have in my office here. Most of these guys, like the aliens and the Jersey devils and whatnot, can be proven. They can be documented, photographed, thrown in a cage, test tube, lab, whatever. If they're out there... maybe. Usually, I don't deal with the stuff you can't prove, like poltergeists or mind control, but that town... yeah, it's got something about it."

Having split his youth between Arondale and the orphanage, Max hardly considered himself geographically savvy about the area. But of course he knew of Twilight Falls, or "TwiFalls." Everyone knew about the place where that Zwieg kid had killed a bunch of classmates.

Dwayne crawled over the backseat, crinkling cut-up newspapers and loose sketchbook pages before huddling by the Twilight Falls section. His stare did the rest of the crawling and he soon happened upon the object of his search, which he pulled from the armrest of the chair, an article—thin, somewhat clear and fresh, not mummified yellow like so many others.

He handed the page to Max. The headline read *Top of his Head, Top of his Game*, by a Marcus Fremont. Despite mediocre photo quality, the subject of the accompanying picture was strikingly familiar.

"That's the guy," Dwayne said. "Clifford Feldman. Don't he look a little like your painting?"

"He does," Max said, mesmerized, pulse racing.

"Think that's your pop?"

"I... I really don't know. Could be."

"I heard this guy was in Twilight Falls, after living in Seattle for a while. The headline got the place wrong—it wasn't San Fran, but they probably just wanted a recognizable locale and all. Plus, I never knew an article that didn't get at least one fact wrong. That's why I do my own investigations."

'You can barely take your eyes off this article.'

"So what drives you, Maximo?" Dwayne asked. "What runs your brush? Besides the missing people, I mean."

A thousand variations of one answer convened in Max's throat, fighting and vying.

"I suppose the unknown," he finally answered. "Like you—kind of. The unknown, unheard, unseen."

"That so?"

"Yeah. To me, that's where inspiration hides, in the world's cracks. And I guess the people who fall into them." He glanced out the window. "I know that also sounded rehearsed. I've said it before."

"You give them a place to fall," Dwayne said.

"Giving them a home," Max said. "That's how I look at it." He brought out a hot sauce packet, bit it, and began pumping the liquid into his mouth.

"Sure thing, sure thing," said Dwayne, unfazed by Max's oral fixation. "You ever have anyone recognize a face? Besides me, I mean?"

"No," Max said curtly. He didn't feel like spilling the recent events of his life to an hour-old acquaintance.

"Listen," Dwayne said. "You're welcome to hitch a ride when I go to Twilight Falls."

"I don't know," Max said.

"That Feldman is having a show up there," Dwayne said. "He's got one at the Peters Museum, going on now, I think, if you want to scope it out."

Max wasn't sure what to say, but was spared the burden of reply by a firm tapping on the driver's side window.

Both men stopped. Through the glass stared a man, red-eyed, hands clawed, mouth ajar as if on the verge of a sneeze. Much of his torso was dirt-streaked and bare save for a ratty strip of cloth he wore like a toga.

He tapped again. "You guys got anything for me?"

Max's heart beat fast.

Dwayne crawled over to the window, rolled it down, and tinkled change into the man's waiting palm.

"Thanks, man," said the man. "Thanks."

When Dwayne turned back, Max gave him a funny look.

"Pretty generous," Max said.

"Like you said, giving them a place to fall."

Again, Max found himself at a loss for reply.

"So what do you say?" Dwayne said.

"To what?"

"To going with me. Up north. The Feldman fellow."

This guy is a psycho, for sure. A killer luring people into his witch's-hut of a van and promising them their dreams and their myths and their legends and their hopes and then... and then....

'Shut up.'

"I'll give you my address and phone number," Max said, getting out a pen. "And I can let you know."

"That's all well and good, Max, but you should know I'm leaving pretty soon. This week, actually. If I'm not mistaken, the show doesn't last much longer."

"That's fine." Max scribbled the info on a discarded sheet of notepaper he found by a cooler.

"But there's someone else who might be interested in joining us."

V

"He's here again."

Karen didn't need to be told. She'd heard his voice, caught a glimpse of him in the entryway — one big, human-shaped nerve. His ego, his esteem, would lay in scattered breadcrumbs for re-gathering on the way back out.

Twice now, this James Cannon had come to The Schoolhouse, wearing his crisp suit as if to impress — the professional preceding the man, a silken layer over his soul. Karen had learned during small talk, vainly contrived to alleviate Cannon's anxiety, that he was a defense attorney.

Figures.

"He's your six-thirty, right?" Danielle asked.

"Yeah, he is." They lounged near the front desk. Down the hall, Monica and Valerie were in separate sessions, one of them moaning loudly between harsh smacks — Monica, probably.

Rose held the door open for James, who entered with a half-formed smile on his face.

Karen waved to him.

"Hi, Penelope," he said.

This time they took the dungeon chamber room.

"So, Mr. Cannon," said Karen in her Penelope twang. "What's on your mind today?"

James laughed a shaky, hiccupping laugh. "I was actually wondering if, um... if I could maybe spank you this time. If not, that's fine, because you're a dominant, right? Not a... um...."

"...submissive?"

"Right right."

"Well, James baby, you just happen to be in luck. I'm a switch."

His hands trembled in his gabardine pockets, between which an observable erection now bulged.

James tried to suppress his excitement. "How old are you?"

"Let's not get bogged down in details," Penelope said, and handed him the paddle. "You got into it just fine the last two times."

"That was because you were spanking *me*."

"It's no big deal, you'll be great." She smiled, but it seemed phony. "Just please don't be too hard." She said this sweetly, melting her face into a cute pout.

Irresistible, he thought. Then her bare ass suddenly and fully appeared before him. Power shuddered through his limbs. He thought of Teresa. She wouldn't be waiting at home with a gourmet feast, not tonight — something to do with her Book Club, probably an excuse. She probably hated him, had begun to despise him. There was relief in that.

Good. Good.

For reasons not wholly understood, James said, "D-did you... did you know I'm an artist?"

"Oh yeah?" she said. "Well, then decorate me however you see fit, James baby."

"Actually, I shouldn't say I am an artist. I sort of was, but I've been looking at my sculptures and thinking about getting back into it."

"Please, James baby, I need some discipline. Bad." She glanced at the clock.

"Could you not call me James baby?" he asked, timidly.

"Okay. Whichever."

"It's nothing against the name. I like it. It's endearing, actually. I just think it's.... You know what? Just say it. Please. Don't mind me."

"This is your castle now. Whatever you want."

"You can call me James baby."

"All right, James baby."

"I wasn't always like this. Please know that. Not this bumbling dork. When I was doing my art—"

His rambling stopped in mid-sentence as Penelope took the paddle from him and gave his own rear a forceful swat.

"Pull 'em down," she commanded. "*Someone's* gonna get it this hour."

Although surprised, James instantly complied.

She walloped him hard. At first, the impacts were spaced well apart, each strike leaving a tingling, ecstatic wake. Then she sped up the rhythm—harder, faster. She smacked away the nerves, she smacked away the guilt, smacked away thoughts of the trial, smacked away the James Cannon of five minutes ago. What remained against the wonderful poundings of pain was that vibratory power, hidden deep in his bones and now emerging further, a corona around his mind.

"Penelope," he said, breathing hard. "Give me the paddle, and get ready."

She grinned and assumed her original position.

"And in fact," James said. "Just to make it more interesting...."

"Yes?"

"Could I maybe tie you up, too?"

Penelope smiled, and it appeared true and bright this time.

Karen had one more client that day, two hours after James Cannon.

She chatted with Monica, who'd had to suck down cigarettes for a client while he tickled her feet. The convulsing reactions of tickle-torture didn't seem too conducive to smoking, but the client's fetish came only in both — as individual actions, they did little for him. Another client required Monica to run around topless in a room full of balloons, bouncing and frolicking.

The girls laughed, and Karen realized in the talk of smoking that she needed a smoke herself.

Not long into her first cigarette, she saw Max coming up the front walk toward the house.

"I need to talk to you," he said. In his hand he held a cutout newspaper article. "Feel like taking a trip up north?"

Chapter 3

I

Norman Ritter missed the crew of Southwest Airlines telling jokes. As two-bit as many of them might have been, they'd provided him good ice-breakers for the trivial schmoozing inherent in openings or art parties. He was also quite appreciative of a chuckle, chintzy or not, when stuck twenty thousand feet above the Earth in a giant cacophonous capsule rank with the breaths, coughs, sneezes, farts, and who-knew-what-else of hundreds of strangers.

Better than spending eight hours in a car.

For much of the flight, he read about Clifford Feldman, easily one of the strangest personalities that had entered his radar. That was saying a lot, too. Although in the last decade Feldman had been quiet about it, in the late seventies he'd claimed to be the latest incarnation of a Count St. Germain, supposedly a legendary alchemist. On live television, he'd demonstrated a method of turning lead into gold, provoking reactions both curious and contemptuous. How had he done it?

He hadn't. A goddamn special effect, as it had turned out. Yet in the swirling limbo of controversy, he'd attracted notoriety, built a platform largely of impressionable, disillusioned flower children. Officially, he never denied his claim of being Germain. Those who wanted to believe... would believe.

They landed in Oakland, and Ritter promptly went to an airport restaurant and grabbed a ham on rye. Nerves had diminished his appetite on the plane, so he ate the sandwich fast on the way to the rental car counter, where they gave him a sparkling blue '89 Buick.

Within an hour, he was on the road north. Not long out of Oakland, he passed a small sign:

Twilight Falls 172 mi.

II

Dead.

The city was dead. The world was dead. His breaths the last, his movement the final, and it was all for good. Death was a process of folding all things and all people inside out, the ultimate reveal of the core principle living in all matter — the sheer grotesquerie unfurled to light once more, everything else a façade.

For the last fifteen hours, Max had been entombed in his cavern. He'd called in sick to work, said he could barely move from his mattress — not altogether false. He was sick, after all, his brain upchucking long-digested memories. Fleeting shades of nightmares hung at the fringes of his mind. His body throbbed with emotions both despised and desired, his soul split between resistance and celebration of these things.

Dwayne had called, and he needed to call him back. Or maybe he didn't. The telemarketer had called next.

Does he care I exist? Sure. Sure. Fine. How are you, sir? Please please *tell me because I'm dying to know.*

They'd head to Northern California on Friday night: he, Karen, and Dwayne. Fifty hours away. *We're all going.* One happy little ridiculous family, smashed haphazardly together in hasty compensation by a cosmos to which he'd long been an afterthought.

Dwayne had said the Feldman show was ending Monday.

Shut up just shut up and be done with it. This is what you've been wanting, right? This is what you've looking for, right? For Christ's sake —

'Shut up!'

Max sifted through his pile of sketchbooks, years and thoughts and sensations all snapshots on the greasy-smudged pages, in the dark-razored lines and light pencil studies. He set them aside, not fully understanding what he was looking for, and took a jar of charcoal dust from a nearby shelf.

He tore off a large sheet of bond paper, spilled the dust upon it, and played in the dark sugar-streaks. His fingers skated across the blackening paper — stormy gray, God crafting a thunderstorm, changing things up here in a white heaven. Max's brain and heart raced one another.

He blew the excess powder off the page, creating an explosive frame, then sat back and looked at it. *Six million dollars, please. Thank you.*

Without washing his hands, he slumped onto his mattress. Between his black fingers he held his small gold cross and, for the first time in nearly six years, issued a silent prayer.

He'd fallen asleep for a while, and awoke to a blurry world.

He awoke—but didn't.

Again he awoke—but didn't.

Ringing – the phone, the phone is ringing – again....

This time he woke up and felt his face, slapped himself, walked toward the sink—then he was back in bed.

Oh God no not again.

He woke up and pulled himself from bed, but he was too heavy and the world was watery. Wavy. His body a sack of concrete. Back in bed.

Okay, this time I'm awake. I'm going to get myself a drink....

No, not awake, not yet, still just below the surface—

Stop ringing!

He screamed but the scream died in his mind.

Someone here there's someone here isn't there what is it what are they.... What is that flying thing is that a moth or a butterfly?

Finally, he managed to surface, to gasp a full conscious breath. The normal weight returned to his limbs, the world becoming sharp and clear and focused once more.

Again, the phone rang.

Thoroughly disoriented and still not entirely convinced he was truly awake, Max staggered to the phone and resurrected his ability to speak. He'd not had an episode of sleep paralysis in over a decade.

"Yo!" Dwayne called on the other end. "I've been trying to get through. You and that girl still on for Friday's trip?"

"Yeah, I'm sorry... just been kinda... never mind." He coughed and cleared his throat, and, in a cracked voice, said, "Yeah, we're still going."

Max exited and the bus pulled lethargically away from the curb, screeching and roaring back onto Venice Boulevard. Lost in himself, he walked with his sketchbook and two newspapers—the *Chicago Sun* and the *Daily Arizona*—tucked firmly under his arm, a plastic Taco Shack bag dangling from two fingers. He only had a few packets left, would have to refill during the night.

At the Sirens Shop, Max relieved Tyler Harris, who sat feet up on the counter while scribbling furiously on a legal pad.

"Any luck with that film festival?" Max asked as he set his things down.

"We haven't submitted yet," Tyler said dryly. Just recently twenty-two, the kid reminded Max of the 'blackies' from Rheta Art College—those not quite Gothic or Punk, but whose wardrobe was one big, black, somber shadow. "You still need to see it. I think you'll like it. Definitely one of my better ones. I wanna turn it into a feature. It sort of reminds me of that one painting you did, a long time ago, that you never sold."

"Rose Clown?"

"Nah, nah, the main shape was like a skull, but it was broken up into like surrealism and cubism, totally trippy. The city in the teeth, the tidal-wave tongue...."

"Ah... Geometric Sk—"

"*Geometric Skull*! That was it!" Tyler clapped his hands. "Yeah, my film's called *Dead Two Walkers*. Zombies with crutches, old people with flamethrowers...

it's awesome. I'll bring it in when I'm done tweaking it."

Max hardly understood the connection between his canvas and what Tyler described, but offered a smile. "Do that."

"All right, dude, I'm off. I'm meeting Sandy for chow."

"Have fun."

"Will do." Tyler gathered up his things and strung his backpack over one shoulder. "Get some good work done tonight."

"Already have."

Outside, the night sank deeper into the city. Max assumed his position behind the counter and tossed Tyler a flippant wave as the kid left the shop.

Almost two hours into his shift, Max had dressed over twenty pages of his sketchbook with faces, both fabricated and real, as well as idle gesture drawings of the occasional customer.

Forty minutes shy of midnight, a man entered, strikingly familiar. Max studied him from the corner of his eye. The man perused the fetish cassettes, his gaze crawling with investigative care over the colorful spines.

Max remembered where he'd seen him. "Can I help you with something?"

"Me? Oh no, I'm fine, just kind of browsing. Seeing what's here."

The man pulled out one of the cassettes, glancing at the front, then the back. He shot a glance over to Max, who smiled. The guy quickly broke eye contact. Like a game of peek-a-boo or something.

The money man, the broker, the banker. What did Karen say his name was? John? Jason?

Max knew the customer also recognized him, but wasn't sure if he'd placed him. "You look familiar. I saw you at The Schoolhouse, didn't I?"

The man steeled. "Did you? The Schoolhouse?"

"Yeah, the club here in Venice. I saw you there last week, didn't I?"

The man hesitated. "I think so. You look familiar, too. Did you have a session there?"

"Yeah," Max said, trying to put the guy's mind at ease. "Yeah, I had a session there."

"Which girl?"

Now Max froze. Why did he even bother speaking? He didn't know the real names of any of the other girls, much less their aliases. So, odd as it felt, the only one he did know came tumbling off his tongue.

"Penelope, really?" said the man. "She's fantastic, definitely the prettiest girl there. She really knows her stuff, on both ends too! Were you a submissive or a dominant? She's a switch, y'know."

"Um, I was a... dominant."

The guy chuckled. "Nice. She's unbearably cute when she's a submissive, but she's so damn sexy when she's dominating you, too. Both sides are sexy but in different ways. She's a genius at the stuff, honestly."

"Glad you enjoyed it."

"Lots of these videos were produced at The Schoolhouse, right?"

"Yup. Most of them."

"Is Penelope in any of them?"

"I don't really know, actually. I think she's too new a face there. She might be in the upcoming videos."

No no but really she's missing, right? She can't go traipsing in front of cameras.

The man asked, "Do you know when those might come in? The new videos?"

"Not sure. I could look it up, or ask Tyler or Danny. They're usually the ones who sign for them. You can always ask them directly, too, whenever you're there."

The man kept looking over the cassette spines. "I'd love to see Penelope in a film. She'd just light up the screen. And it's not just her smile or that... kind of bad-girlness she exudes, but the way she bubbles over with character."

"What's your name?" Max asked, now gesture-sketching the man and the space around him.

"James. Yours?"

"I'm Max."

With a playful salute, James said, "Good to meet you."

"You know, it's too bad for the rest of us," Max said. "Penelope has a boyfriend."

"Oh?"

"Yeah, lucky guy, huh?"

"Yes... yes, very much so." James rubbed his chin. "How do you know? Do you talk to her outside The Schoolhouse?"

"Kind of. We talk during her sessions, sometimes during her breaks."

James gestured toward Max's sketchbook. "That's nice. Do you draw her at all? Or any of the girls there?"

"Not really."

"I haven't drawn in so long, but I've always loved art. I know some people who know some people, though, and I also still have connections from my own short-lived days as an artist. I could probably get you a big showing."

"That'd be great."

"Yeah, we could invite anyone and everyone, get you exposed. That's where it is." James stared hard at him. "Anyone you know could come."

The two men fell silent, the space of their conversation filled now by the soft rough scratch of Max's sketching.

A show. Wow. Nice. Is this guy serious?

He certainly looked like he had the cash for it, probably because he bullshitted for a living, and bullshitters made the most. They also... well... bullshitted, so who knew how authentic this James was.

Moments later, James presented Max his purchase: a cassette of The Basement. *Mad Dr. Spankenstein!* screamed the back cover, *has kidnapped and shackled in his dungeon basement a trove of lovely 'assistants.' How will they get out? Or can they?*

James gave Max his card. "Call me, and we'll talk," he said with rubber enthusiasm.

"Thanks."

"Can I see what you were drawing?" James asked, craning his neck around to get a better view of the sketchbook. "Is that me?"

"Yeah, I was just warming up," Max said.

"Cool. See, that's what I want to be able to do, capture that one spark of life, that jazz, so quickly. The best ones can always do it fast. They're like artistic short-order cooks."

With a thoughtful nod, Max approved the phrase. He handed James his change and the receipt and the bag that now contained the man's new private fantasy. He tried not to think about what went on with those videos and with the people who bought them, but his imagination was too slippery. He would drown the unwanted imagery in sketch.

"Take it easy," James said, scooping up his purchase. "Maybe I'll see you at The Schoolhouse."

III

Dwayne pulled up to the curb outside Higgins' apartment complex. God, he wanted to leave. *Frickin' downtown Los Angeles, the stinking urban entrails of the city.* He was reminded of New York and... and....

No, stop. Don't think about her now. Later.

From the entrance alcove burned the eyes of a small man in a black derby and tattered overcoat. They watched one another.

Higgins was due any moment.

Dusk moved in, twinkling pores opening in the sky, seven stars visible—not bad for a big city. Astronomy had always been a keen interest of Dwayne's, but, for lack of time and money, he did little else beyond taking occasional glimpses through his old portable telescope—useful in the star-splattered desert sky—and casual trips to various observatories. His UFO studies, involving as they did information on star distances, light years, comets, wormholes and such, made for a sufficient compromise.

All that good shit, as Jenny used to say.

The derby man watched Dwayne, and Dwayne watched him. Something small scurried under a dumpster just behind the complex, a rat, most likely.

Somewhere close, a siren wailed. Dwayne stared motionless at his dashboard, where a color copy of John Baxter's famous watercolor depiction of the Dover Demon stared a dead orange soul back at him.

The Dover Demon remained on his list. No sightings of it had been made public for nearly thirteen years now. It had probably been nothing more than an interdimensional traveler just passing through. In either case, it would be worth a stay in Massachusetts, whenever he got to the area. Who knew when that would be?

Next on his list, after Twilight Falls, and once he'd sold a few more pieces in L.A., were the giant birds spotted in Washington and Vancouver, the supposed inspiration for Native American thunderbird lore. Something about them fascinated him—those and UFOs. Maybe it was the sky, that great abyss above us. Only, unlike the sea, it didn't really end.

He wondered what he might chase afterward.

He also knew that, sometime before he completed this job, he would have to come clean to Max Higgins.

Movement near his van pulled Dwayne from his thoughts. Higgins approached, toting a single black duffel bag and wearing the same clothes in which Dwayne had met him—paint-ridden jeans and a worn flannel shirt, with a navy-blue undershirt.

"Open up," Max said.

Dwayne unlocked all the van doors and his guest clambered in.

"Where should I put this?" Max asked, holding up his bag. "Just under the seat?"

"Sure, that's fine. It'll fit."

Max nestled into the front seat, buckled up, and sighed long and hard.

"You're late, Maximo," Dwayne said in dry humor. "Not by much, of course. Everything all right?"

"Eh, yeah, everything's fine."

"Hmm?"

"There's a huge part of me that says this trip is a bad idea." Max ran his hand through his hair. "But I don't know. I don't know what I feel anymore."

Dwayne maneuvered the van back into the city's concrete bloodstream. "Keep in mind, Max, that you don't know for sure if this guy is really your father."

"Looks just like him."

"Lots of people look like each other. Take a look in the Coincidences and Miracles section of volume three of *The Unexplained*, if you don't believe me."

"'Course I know there's a chance it's not him, but so many things seem to click into place, and I don't even think I can explain how. The man in that article, the man in my painting... I feel like... I feel like I'm the subject of someone's sketch, slowly coming together, filling out—trapped in a new world."

"What about this woman we're getting?"

"Karen? What about her?"

"I dunno. She get the same sorta feeling, too? She's your sister, you said?"

"Half-sister, supposedly." Max dug into his pocket and retrieved a Taco Shack packet.

"Where are we going, by the way?" Dwayne merged onto the I-10 freeway. "Where's this chick live?"

"Santa Monica, just off Pico. I'll show you when we get closer. For now, just get off at Overland."

Dwayne drifted through traffic with jerky lane changes, random punch-bursts of acceleration, the windows moving oil canvases of the city and all its glittering stipples.

On reaching Karen's complex, they climbed out and headed upstairs to her door. Two knocks and seconds later, they were staring at a strange man.

"Yes?"

Max spoke. "Yeah, is... is Karen around?"

"Karen? Think you got the wrong apartment, dude."

"Vivian's roommate."

"Oh." The guy's eyes widened. "Oh, okay. No, she's not here, I don't think, but hold on. Vivian!"

From behind a bathroom door and the running shower, Vivian called back, "Yeah?"

"Karen! Where is she?"

"What?"

"Where is Karen?"

The guy left the door, headed toward the bathroom, and promptly returned. "She said Karen's at work."

"Work?" Max said. "Thought she'd be off by now."

The man shrugged. Behind him, Vivian emerged wrapped in a towel, skin glistening, wet curly hair like a pile of corkscrew pasta.

"Some client called for her," Vivian said. "Made a special appointment. She told me to tell you to pick her up there."

"Well, when's she going to be done?"

"Don't think it'll be more than an hour. Her appointment's at nine o'clock. It's... what... almost 9:30 now. Who knows, she might be through with it by now." Vivian squeezed the towel tighter around her. "I'm kind of disappointed, too, actually. We were s'posed to use up this weed my cousin hooked me up with, before she got the call."

"Call?"

"Yeah, from work. Dude wanted her for a session. Paid double for her to be there." She shrugged. "I don't know."

"All right," Max said. "Thanks."

"Sure thing."

The man closed the door, and Dwayne and Max set off down the stairs.

With wide arms and lustful zeal, James greeted Teresa, who, caught pleasantly off guard, more than reciprocated. Their lovemaking hadn't been like this in years, a resurgent flame of their initial courting. Teresa couldn't even remember those times being as good.

When subtly prodded about this renewed enthusiasm, James just smiled and answered in kisses.

"Do you mind if we use handcuffs or ropes?" he said at one point.

"What?"

"Handcuffs or ropes," he said. "Maybe liven things up?"

She furrowed her brow, unsure if he was joking. "I... no, I don't think so. Sorry."

Something fell in his eyes. "No problem."

PART TWO

"A town is a colonial animal."
~ John Steinbeck

Chapter 4

I

"This the Jersey Devil?" Karen asked.

She leaned forward, holding one of Dwayne's personal photo albums and pointing to a blurry picture of a forest and a road and a tall, horse-like figure. The photo had been snapped at dusk, but the camera had caught a glint of the animal's eye, creating a pivot point around which to spin into view the rest of its murky, silhouetted shape.

Eyes on the road, Dwayne darted a brief glance at the album, needing only one glance to recall the account.

Max sat in the passenger seat, shifting gazes from himself in the side mirror to the black California terrain sliding up from the sea and away toward the night.

"I think so," Dwayne said. "I mean, I thought him to be the devil at the time. Truth be told, I don't know what it was—could've been a moose or something. It was dark."

"Doesn't really look like a moose to me."

"Nor to me, and it certainly didn't look like a moose when it moved off, but I can never be sure. Tracking down the things I do, your whole experience is like a funhouse, one annoying deceptive lead after another, running into glass."

"The Jersey Devil is supposed to have wings, right?"

"It is," Dwayne said with a chuckle. "Though all sorts of things have been misidentified as the Devil, even cougars. You're from the area, right? The East?"

"East Coast? Yeah. I remember my mother told me about it when I was four, when we were in New Jersey. Of course, I thought I saw it everywhere."

"Where you from again?"

Both Karen and Max replied, "Baltimore."

"So, you a conspiracy buff, too?" Max said to Dwayne.

With a single chuckle, Dwayne said, "No, I'm not. You search this van, you won't find any of that stuff—no moon-landing theories, no Masonry, no JFK. Some UFOs, sure, but my targets go beyond conspiracy. I love the monsters because they're untouched by us. There's peace in that. They're in a world outside the petty noisy one we cooked up. What does Bigfoot care if Oswald really pulled the trigger? Peace. That's *peace*."

"Or you could just light up," Karen said, mock-holding a joint, dragging air.

"You're on your own there," said Max.

"What do you mean by that?" Karen asked.

"Nothing. Never mind."

"No," said Dwayne. "What's up, Maximo?"

"Well, I've never done any drug, and don't plan to."

"You smoke," said Karen.

"Used to, but you know what I mean."

"Nothing wrong with that, Max," she said. "It's all overrated anyway. I wish I could remember my junior and senior years. They're supposedly the best of high school."

"Yeah," said Max. "And as long as we're at it, I might as well spill the fact that I'm a virgin, too."

"A virgin?" Dwayne said. "Don't you work at a sex shop?"

"And...?"

"Just uh... find that a little ironic, is all. And funny. No offense."

"None taken."

"It's strange, Max..." Karen said.

"What is?"

"You and me, our reactions to our mothers."

"Our mothers?"

"Yeah. We both had very religious mothers, and we both let them influence our lives in extremes. Your mother's shield stunted your willingness to try anything outside the realm of her permission, like she had some sort of permanent guilt machine installed in you that beeped and went nuts anytime you were tempted.

"Me, on the other hand... I went all out rebelling against my mom — snuck out to parties, had sex, did drugs, all sorts of shit. I think I was doing it as sort of a punishment to her. Maybe I blamed her for dad's disappearance, I don't know. But when I got in trouble, I spat it in her face. Then she sent me away to school and I ran away and haven't looked back since."

"Goddamn," Dwayne said. "There a happy story to tell in either of your lives?"

"Sure," Karen answered. "Just hasn't really been told yet."

"I remember I always questioned my mom, sort of," Max said. "I was shy about saying a lot of it out loud, so a lot of it I just thought. I felt so much of what she spouted was wrong, but I didn't know why. I was so young. I'm surprised I even felt as strongly as I did."

Dwayne stole a glance at him. "You an atheist, Maximo?"

"No. Atheism is a copout, too."

"Okay."

"I never understood the big heehaw over evolution versus creationism, either," Max said. "To me it's simple: evolution proves God."

"How's that?" Dwayne asked.

"Creating anything is a long and arduous process of trial and error. You never know where a piece is truly going to end up. Question is, was all this a surprise to God? And was it a good surprise? And if it wasn't, I doubt it turned out as well as it looked in God's head. Perfection is always shackled inside your skull. Think of all the Earth's mass extinctions, wiping out everything to start anew — going back to the drawing board. Just reminds me of myself when I crumple up a crappy sketch and start again."

"So I take it the whole God-is-perfect idea doesn't factor in?"

"No. He isn't perfect. He's made some good stuff, but He isn't perfect. Still taking lessons."

For a long period thereafter, no one said anything. After several miles of self-conscious fidgeting, Karen asked if they could pull over so she could smoke.

II

Norman Ritter felt a new energy here, one he'd never felt before.

For years, Twilight Falls had been a bold point on the art-world map. Although he'd been here several times, there was something different about the place today. It sat on the edge of its seat, prickly and aware, as though anticipating a grand event. Ritter was not a very spiritual person—he left belief in such things as auras and spirits to his wife, Angelica, and the likes of artists he covered—but something in the air of this town pressed on him., Though reluctant to use the term, he could only describe the sensation as *weird vibes*.

The Feldman Naturalism show had been going on for a while but had not been widely publicized. He would be getting in late on the action, his preference, as it usually proved the most interesting to him. Expectations always ran high at a show's beginning, stories and speculation abounding in the enticing newness of it all.

This late into the game, however, after weeks of circulating discussion, true opinions tended to emerge, a consensus more definable. Ritter liked to capture that, a glimpse into the work's true resonance. But who really knew anything? Prediction in art was a fool's errand.

He'd arrived in Twilight Falls in the early evening and checked into the Morning Light Bed & Breakfast. Had to love the sign: *We Make Your Stay Shine!* over a cartoon sun sporting large hokey sunglasses. Darkly amusing, too, given this had been the scene of that schoolteacher's double homicide in the seventies. Amazed it even remained in business, Ritter figured perhaps they'd gotten by on local, residential loyalty and, frankly, outsiders like himself who sought a little morbidly curious comfort.

His room, polished and pristine, had a nice queen-sized bed, a crisp floral design motif, unexpectedly large bathroom, and comfortable-looking lounge chairs by the window.

After unpacking, he called Angelica. The phone rang and rang, until the answering machine picked up.

Where is she? Sleeping? Bathroom?

"Hey, Angel," he said. "Hope you're keeping off your feet. Just letting you know I'm safe and settled in. Love you."

Lately, Angie had been feeling tight twinges, pains in her lower abdomen. With little more than a month left in her pregnancy, the situation worried him—more so when she was out of reach, when *they* were out of reach.

He hung up, then headed out for some exploration and possibly an early dinner.

The cold air grew colder still when the ocean-scented breeze picked up. Ritter forced himself to walk faster, get that circulation going. The sky smeared with gray, like newsprint sealed-over the town. He passed coffee shops, used bookshops, flower shops, antiques, a diner.

The people don't look at me.

Submerged in their own world, they weren't exactly of the charming, gregarious, small-town type. A town full of artists, maybe, like those two impossibly young novelists who'd just debuted on the New York Times bestseller list, Martin Becker or John Smith, or... something like that. They were only half a decade out of high school, he'd read.

Everyone's head seemed in the clouds. Ritter mused they were all the high-dreaming, funny runoff filtered over from San Fran, up from LA, down from Portland, and from God-only-knew where else.

III

To their right sprawled dark hills and valleys, lonely in gloom though falling far short of the primordial blackness of the ocean to their left. The moon remained absent.

Under the van's wan light, Karen leafed through loose papers found on the floor, reading the text, looking at the pictures but not really absorbing anything—not really, not with these things scratching at her mind. She'd wanted out of her life back east, out of all of it, and she had done it. Clean break. She hadn't belonged there.

Yet here, with Max, her life afloat in fragments, she belonged all too well and that frightened her just as much.

Max dozed in the passenger seat. He still didn't know the full story behind Dwayne.

Should he ever know? Why? Because it's inevitable.

She had orchestrated this; they would only become more and more entwined, forcing such secrets into closer proximity, giving them progressively less room to hide.

Maybe he's not who I think he is. Maybe he's not my brother and I'm not deceiving him.

Karen looked at the papers in her hand, grainy photocopies of some kind of text accompanied by pictures of bizarre flora, some resembling mutated cornstalks, others with gaping mouths like Venus flytrap.

Dwayne kept one hand on the wheel and, with the other, flipped stuttering through the radio stations, giving jockeys and singers mere seconds to prove their worth.

Karen stared through the windshield at the several yards of lit road ahead of them, at the night melted over the land.

Dwayne clicked off the dial and the van's guttural purr took over. "What you got there?" he asked in a lowered voice.

"What?" Karen said, still staring ahead.

"Those papers... that the Voynich manuscript?"

"Oh... I don't know. I was just looking through whatever was here. I'm sorry if I messed anything up."

"This whole van needs a major cleanup. Don't worry about it."

"What are these?"

"Those are photocopies of the Voynich manuscript I got from a fellow I know at Harvard, someone who worked with one of the linguists involved in trying to crack the code. So far, no one's gotten anything. Written in a totally incomprehensible language."

"Strange."

"You're telling *me*."

"What about all the plant drawings?"

"Your guess is as good as mine."

"Hmm."

"Yeah, actually, interesting we're going to Twilight Falls," Dwayne said. "Because it was a Native American tribe that supposedly lived around there that shed any kind of light on the subject. Code-breakers found distant similarities between characters in their language and those in the Voynich. Makes little sense to me, though, since the Voynich manuscript was written in the thirteenth century by a European named Roger Bacon."

"What was the tribe?"

"The Agras."

"Agras. I've never heard of them." Karen snorted. "Didn't help that I never paid attention in history, though."

"Can't imagine you would have. Heard of them, I mean. They've been overshadowed by the Agra Circle. Don't know much about them but I know enough to stay away. They're a cult, basically, based loosely on whatever they thought the Agras believed. In fact, some scholars are skeptical even of the real tribe's existence, thinking maybe it was PR for the Circle.

"The original tribespeople, as I understand it," Dwayne continued, "were supposedly Aztecan descendants who migrated north after the Spanish conquest. They settled somewhere up here. Weren't that many of them. Their practices and spirituality and all that totally changed. Basic tenet of their culture was that the gods had stowed away inside them, to escape persecutors. The tribesmen were supposed to unleash them, re-birth their gods, generation by generation. Guess gestation and delivery time is long for a god."

"Or maybe it's the blink of an eye," Karen said, "by God standards."

"Hah, maybe." Dwayne nodded. "My favorite thing is their paradigm for how things happen."

"What do you mean? Happen how?"

"Anyway, anytime, anywhere. The four elements we know — air, fire, water, earth — but the Agras also had more intangible forces at work. There was a destroyer, a creator, a collector, and a teacher. The destroyer was the bookend of the process, destroying first so the creator could create, and the creator would create with the tools and the knowledge gathered by the collector. The teacher would then spread the seed of the creation. It was never such a linear process, but they believed everything happened with those four forces operating together, in whatever capacity necessary."

"So not just one of each?"

"No, could be tons of them. There's no one *any* of them. They're all collective, I think, lots of creators, destroyers, collectors, teachers."

"Interesting."

"It works if you think about it. Think of how this country kicked off, destroying native societies, creating new colonies, expeditions like Lewis and Clark collecting what they could, paving the way, and word of all this progress spreading and inspiring yet more of it, more destruction, for even more creation, more collection. Clanking on and on."

When Max stirred in the front seat, Dwayne gave him a friendly pat on the shoulder. "Good sleep, Maximo?"

"I guess. Just had a dream that I knew was a dream and was telling myself to remember when I woke up, but...."

"Gone?"

"Yep. Blinked away."

"Hate when that happens."

Max riffled through his pocket and brought out a Taco Shack packet. He bit it open and began sucking it like an infant on a pacifier.

Max drifted as for miles the dark quiet of the surrounding area filled the van—no voices, Max sucking taco-sauce packets, Dwayne in a red-eyed meditation with the wheel, the road guzzled by the headlights. Karen stared out the window at things emerging from the gloom.

Then the sign appeared: *Pfeiffer Big Sur*.

"Oh, Big Sur," Karen said. "We should stop and camp for the night."

"What?" said Max.

"Not for real," she said with a playful punch on his bicep. "Maybe on the way back down."

"I don't know."

"Hey, Karen," said Dwayne.

"What's up?"

"Could you reach back in the cooler there and get the jar of cookies out?"

"Sure."

"I think we can hang out for a little while," Dwayne said as he pulled to the side of the road, gravel crunching. "I need a good stretch anyway, and it wouldn't be a California road trip without some nature."

"Here." Karen handed him the jar, which looked to be full of small oatmeal cookies.

Dwayne shut off the engine and nature burst all around them, echoing with insects chirping and buzzing, the wind moving like a conspiratorial whisper among the ragged, silhouetted pines.

"We're not going to be here long, right?" Max asked.

"No. Just taking a stretch. Won't be long."

Max was about to get out when Dwayne tilted the cookie jar at him, and he took one. He opened the door and, in a cold grip, the air took his skin. He stuck the cookie in his mouth as he fetched his duffel bag and pulled on his sweatshirt.

Nearby, Karen munched on her cookie. She'd undone her ponytail, collapsing her golden hair to her shoulders.

"They're kind of dry," Max said. "What are these cookies?"

Dwayne took a bite of his own and stared off into the sky, which, unimpeded by big city lights, now stretched its starry cosmic legs—the Milky Way a misty belt, ancient wisdom winking down.

"They're whatever you want them to be," Dwayne said.

A short time later, the ground became something like liquid.

It undulated beneath Max, rippled, melted back into some mold newly pliable by God's dissatisfied hands. There were bubbles, too, bubbles of grass and soil surfacing and popping, tearing little holes in the fragile spacetime about him.

The dark ground and the dark forest and the dark sky bled together, hugged him, *breathed* on him—the wind the fresh mint-breath of Mother Nature. Calming, but so close—like any mother, so goddamn suffocatingly *close*, knowing him too well, sifting through the disarrayed album of his memories and thrusting them at him from long-dusty corners.

Max tried to steady himself.

"What's going on? What the hell is happening?"

"Max?" Karen said.

"All right there, Maximo?" Dwayne asked.

Oh no, but it was the *woods*, for God's sake—the woods, but they looked cartoony and two-dimensional now, like the graphics of a videogame... and things, ill-defined, indefinable things, the enemy of all rationality. Overhead, the moon grew porous then began to liquefy, cascading down the gold-specked night, pooling into a ghost-glow beyond the trees.

Max closed his eyes, body heaving with breath.

Dwayne chuckled. "Relax, Maximo. They're just special cookies, taking us on a little detour."

"The goddamn *moon* just melted."

"He might be a bad tripper," Karen said to Dwayne. "Maybe this was a bad idea...."

"Well, can't do anything about it right now. But that's why I made small ones."

"How long does this last?" Max shouted.

"Not too long. Don't worry, Maximo. They're safe. I know my guy."

"Your guy?"

"Yeah. We took 'em too."

"This is insane. You fucking *drugged* me."

"You can paint it but you sure can't take it, huh? Whoa!" Dwayne backed up, waving at some mirage of his own.

For another half-hour, the world wore various masks, became a kite guided by the shifting winds of sensation and emotion. Max slumped into a nearby clearing, mumbling for it all to go away as he pinched the gold cross around his neck.

Karen sat on the van's bumper, smoky seahorses curling from the cigarette between her fingers.

Approaching footsteps... Dwayne. "How you doing?" he said.

Karen shook her head. "I'm all right. Just entranced by colors right now."

"I can see that," he said. "He's going to be okay, by the way."

She nodded this time. "He will. We will. I need this. He needs this."

"Certainly seem to know him pretty well already."

"I don't know, I wouldn't necessarily say that. He's walled off. Typical artist type, maybe. But it's all right there, all visible, no matter how much he tries to hide it or wall it off, at least to me. It's like a messy room: nothing's put away, but it's all there for you to pick up if you just rummage a bit."

Dwayne nodded.

"I can't explain it very well," Karen said. "I have an almost instinctive hobby of analyzing people. And he *is* my brother. There is *something* there. I'm not crazy."

"I know you're not crazy," Dwayne said. "Any crazy person wouldn't have hired me."

"Kind of funny," Karen said, exhaling smoke.

"What is?"

"Think tonight was the first time I've heard him curse."

"Wow — observant. Might put me out of a job."

"Remember, I absorb people. I notice all kinds of things. I noticed tonight you turned your hat forward for the first time since I've known you."

Dwayne laughed again. "Which hasn't been long, either."

Silence for another moment.

"Hey, listen," Dwayne said. "Would you mind if I snoozed for a little while? Just to recharge the batteries?"

"Fine with me." Karen held up her cigarette. "I prefer my fiery death be slow and painful."

"We can drive on into TwiFalls in the early morning. Think I can sell Max on it?"

They looked over at Max sitting in the clearing, arms clutching his knees, head cast down into the shadow of his groin.

Karen made her way over toward him, then turned back to Dwayne with a hesitant smile. "Let me tell him," she said. "Go ahead and get some sleep."

IV

Dwayne slept for several hours, awakening to misty, predawn dusk. He stirred in his seat. The movement sent a ripping pain up his back, and he winced and groaned.

"You all right there?" Max said. A sketchbook lay sprawled across his lap, marked up with a frenzy of drawings.

"Hey," Dwayne croaked. In the back, Karen lay curled up, asleep. "You been up all this time, Maximo?"

"I have."

"Oh that's right, you slept earlier."

"Yeah." There was something beneath Max's words.

"How are you doin'?" Dwayne asked through a yawn.

"Other than the fact that two people I'm on a road trip with drugged me? I think I'm pretty damned all right."

"Look, Max, I'm sorry about that."

"Whose idea was it, anyway?"

"It was an impulse. I've had those cookies for a while now. My friend in Tennessee knows a guy who bakes 'em. I just figured it'd be a good opportunity, with us in the van. And for you to get, I don't know, inspiration or something."

"Don't need any."

"Finding it on the page there?"

"Yes and no." Max drew a few loose lines.

Dwayne didn't say anything. He wanted to tell Max to let out whatever was behind those eyes, but held back out of fear of the result. He sensed thousands of sleeping vipers in Max Higgins.

"You get a good rest?"

"Yeah, I did," Dwayne said. "I'm ready to hit the road if you are. I'd say we got about another hour before we hit TwiFalls. I should stop and get gas, too. Pup's thirsty."

Dwayne started the engine and pulled back onto the highway.

Max rubbed his forehead. Like a gluttonous eater unable to entertain more food, he now looked at his sketchbook with similar disgust. Dozens of drawings and gesture-sketches crowded the white space. Having whipped through his mind, they'd burst from his fingers and struck the page in a stillborn thud—not a word, no music, no *song*. He'd short-circuited something in himself.

Dr. Farmer had said his artistic output was a way to flush out *the demons*, ironically using the same terminology as his mother: an exorcising. A healthy notion, sure, but, as Farmer had said, ultimately no good if Max were just relaying this darkness into the world uncritically, without self-reflection, the lack of which might corrode him surely as running water might eventually corrode metal.

You don't want to drive it away.

Eyes stinging, he closed the sketchbook. He shivered under his sweatshirt and so reached over and cranked up the heat. "Hope you don't mind."

"Not at all," Dwayne said, eyes fixed on the road.

The dawn fanned out across the sky, a shining pink aura for the forest. As the van sped along, the dusk gave way to a harsh yellow light, the newborn sun pushing up from the horizon.

Fifteen miles from Twilight Falls, they pulled into a rustic gas station at the base of a small mountain.

"Grey's Peak," Dwayne said. "Think that's the name of this place. It's haunted by a Bigfoot-type creature who apparently guards a door to another dimension."

Karen snorted. "Find the door yet?"

"Oh, I already found it," Dwayne said, grinning. "Just gotta find my way *back* now."

Max climbed out and visited the restroom.

Karen got out to stretch, popping her back.

Near the restroom, two men in straw hats and flannel shirts sat in plastic lawn chairs, soil-born spectators, one pot-bellied and one skinny, almost like an old-time comic duo.

Dwayne filled up the tank and went in to pay, the clerk uttering robotic gratitude. He turned to leave when something caught his eye on the nearby bulletin board. Through a shrub of flyers and cards stared a pair of familiar eyes. He lifted the papers to get a better look, snatched one sheet, and walked out.

Back from the bathroom, Max waited now in the passenger seat, door open as he sketched the two men in the chairs.

Karen climbed into the middle seat.

"Making us look good?" the larger man said to Max.

Max gave a quick salute, a weak smile on his lips.

"All right then. You sell that and become Piccasser and you send us a little something, right?"

Max just nodded. Dwayne came out of the station and gave a thumbs-up that everything was good to go.

Max closed his sketchbook and shut his door.

As Dwayne climbed into the driver's seat, he pulled the folded piece of paper from his breast pocket and handed it to Max. "Thought you might get a kick out of this. Found it hanging up in there."

The paper featured a long-faced, black-and-white portrait of Christ, similar to the many that used to hang in Cynthia Higgins' household. Above the picture sat a bold, familiar word: *Missing*.

"Kind of amusing, huh?" Dwayne said.

Max stared at it. This very portrait used to unsettle him, not fill him with any sort of divine comfort—the Wood Christ, as he'd come to call it. The eyes were slanted and melancholic, mouth agape, the stiff rigidity of the pose so... well, wooden.

Max folded the paper and slipped it into his sketchbook.

The drive was beginning to wear on him. This van had been his home for the last three weeks, it seemed. He was shackled to it, enslaved to this diesel destiny, chugging headlong into uncertainty. Insanity. It had been centuries since his last shower, and his skin felt like a prickly dance floor for mites and bugs.

On the first leg up Grey's Peak, no one said anything.

Soon the trees parted, unveiling a town miles below on the other side. Nestled in a small valley, it was a splash of society, dropped into the wilderness. It appeared not so much the conquering host of the surrounding woods as a guest, well-acclimated, even welcomed.

A palpable energy struck Max, a sensation that, to his mind's eye, resembled heatwaves shimmering off a desert.

"There we are," Dwayne said. "Twilight Falls."

Chapter 5

I

Patronage of the Feldman show was impressive, the Peters Museum swollen with suits and dresses, people moving in currents of mumbling gossip, a miasma of opinion. Norman Ritter moved among them. He'd forgone the earlier VIP press-only showing, preferring not to have the stink of media on him. He'd report from the trenches.

On an odyssey around the exhibit, Ritter found these so-called "Neo-Naturalist" works warranting mere licks, not bites. To him, art shows were psycho-spiritual buffets. Most pieces, his eyes would just lick — a fleeting sample of flavor. Others would warrant a bite, a more considerable taste, something you could sink your teeth into.

Yet here, he found little meat in which to dig his critical canines — stick figures, chalky eyes, squiggles... art's sparse appetizers before the overstuffed entrees of the classical and Renaissance eras.

There were also things not even prehistoric man, in his limited wonder, would have classified as art, however he might have defined it: urine-soaked rocks, plaster casts of naked feet, stacks of rocks, crude tools fashioned from wood and stone, like the spear hung in the north wing attributed to a Daniel Marbury, branch manager of a Wells Fargo Bank in town.

Much of the exhibit was mock cave art. Given Ritter's loose familiarity with the work, he assumed it a quirky homage to the origins of the creative mind, to the species' first Rembrandts, showing, tongue firmly in cheek, the strides humankind had made in technique and vision.

He noticed the sign:

After 40,000 years, Art still asks the same Questions.

"Excuse me, sir?"

Ritter turned to a boy of college age, with black spiky hair and clad in a suit one size too big.

"Are you a member of the press?" the boy said.

Ritter wrinkled his brow. *Goddammit, just leave me alone!*

"I am, yes."

"What outlet, may I ask?"

"*Direct Canvas*. It's a magazine."

"Oh, of course. Los Angeles, right?"

Ritter nodded.

"Did you know Clifford Feldman is going to make an appearance tonight?"

"That's what I hear."

"Along with our other featured artists. You picked a good day to come."

"Who are you, exactly?"

The boy smiled. "I'm working on it."

What?

"Would you like to interview any of the featured artists?" the boy asked.

Ritter checked his watch. There was a glazed detachment in the boy's eyes, a moist idealism that bothered him. "Sure. I'd appreciate that."

"Mr. Feldman isn't available right now. He will be, though. I don't know who you're most interested in talking to but—"

"Any of them would be fine," Ritter said.

"Let me check on either Krauford or Wilson, see if I can't scrounge them up for you."

"Thank you."

"Thank *you*." The kid moved away, enveloped in the night-fragments of formalwear.

Ritter idled in the corner, near a velvet rope cordoning off a rock. A *rock*... uprooted from the soil, still caked with mud and dirt and stringy roots and even sporting tiny, visible bugs. The lithic surface had been decorated with the crude, chalky likeness of a human figure and a shape that resembled a butterfly.

"Sir?"

The boy and his brisk return.

"Yes?"

"Mr. Wilson is willing to conduct an interview with you. If you'd like, I can bring you to him."

"Well, where is he?"

"You can meet him in the lounge of the TwiFalls Inn over on Keller Avenue and Eighth. I've told him you're coming. Is that okay?"

"That's fine." He glanced around the show floor. "You'll be able to drive me there?"

The boy nodded furiously.

In the few steps between the museum and the car, part of Norman Ritter wanted to run away, never to be seen or heard from again.

Max had been quiet for some time, finding little to

talk about.

Karen leaned forward and peered through the drizzle-dotted windshield. "Where are the falls?"

"There's a canyon just beyond the town," Dwayne said. "Right over that way. You can't see it well from here, but they're about a fifteen-minute hike in."

Fog dressed the air, obscuring Max's view of the town, though he kept watch as the van rumbled lonely down the winding mountain. A clocktower jutted from the center of town, at the northwestern base of which spread a residential labyrinth mingled with the evergreens of the bordering forest.

"Anyone notice we haven't seen another car for a while?" Max said.

"It's a bit of a hidden place," said Dwayne. "That's sort of its charm. It's a popular spot with artists. I know why, too."

"Why?" Max said.

"There's a magnetism here, a gravity. It's a brothel of muses, this place. I don't know why. I don't know if it's bullshit and all suggestion, or if there's really something here. I don't care. I just know it always gets me going. And I'm feeling it already, that itch. What about you?"

"Not feeling any itch," Max said, watching the window. "And I've haven't heard that about Twilight Falls."

Dwayne shoved a stick of gum into his mouth. "Well, as you once put it to me, inspiration hides in the unknown, unseen, unheard."

II

In many places, Max had encountered the phrase *bustling small town*, but had never experienced such a sight for himself, not in any California area and certainly not in quiescent Arondale. Yet "bustling" was quite an apt description of this heart of Twilight Falls. People walked, ran, strolled, biked, chatted on a bed of palpable energy. They existed in some sort of matrix, all things precise and calculated. There was a rhythm to it all, almost a contrivance, as if all this were staged.

"This place is strange," Max said. "I feel like we're driving into a rehearsal for a play."

"Funny how crowded this section is, huh?" said Dwayne. "Downtown is a million times different than the rest of town."

"Where's the Peters Museum?"

"I think it's on Kingston Avenue and Sixth."

"You know where that is?"

"Yeah, I've been there before. Always need a little refresher, though."

They rolled onto a street toward the town's quieter residential limbs, the electric buzz of downtown simmering. As they drove, Dwayne played occasional tour guide. Along the way they saw signs promoting the Peters' Neo-Naturalism show, as well something called the "Mind Splash Festival."

"It's a fairly new thing, I think," Dwayne said of Mind Splash. "Kind of an urban Burning Man, minus the giant... well... burning man."

"Not sure how that'd work," Karen said.

They turned on Kingston and traveled four and a half blocks before reaching the Peters Museum, a square brown building more resembling a high school gym. Dwayne pulled up alongside a red curb and idled with the engine running.

"Here we are. What's the plan, folks?"

"Well, we have some time, don't we?" Karen said. "Before Feldman is supposed to show?"

"I actually don't know exactly when that is—I think in the early evening sometime. I'm sure they'll tell you up there, but I actually have something I gotta do here, if you both don't mind...."

"What's that?" Max asked.

"It's just... something. It's a long story, kind of a tradition when I come here, and I'd prefer to do it alone. It won't take long—well, I *hope* it won't take long—so if you don't mind I think I'll drop you off here for now."

Dwayne kept his eyes on the road ahead.

Max had a fleeting but terrible vision of him peeling out and leaving them stranded in this weird little burg.

"You're not coming to the museum later?" Karen asked. She seemed bothered by the unexpected announcement, almost in a personal way.

"I will, there's just... something I want to get over with." Dwayne flicked his head back and forth. "As I said, it's something I do when I come here. Why don't you two take a stroll around town? There's enough sketch fodder here for years, Maximo."

There was an autumn in Dwayne's eyes, and the usually humorous *Maximo* came out in melancholy breath.

"Okay...."

"You'll be here?" Dwayne asked.

"Most likely," Karen said.

"I don't want to stay long," Max said.

Max nodded. "I'll be around, don't worry. Errand shouldn't take too long."

"All right."

"You have enough to get in?" Dwayne asked. "For the two of you?"

Both checked, nodded.

"Okay then, see you guys a little later."

Max and Karen retrieved a few things and climbed out of the van, slamming the two doors in thunderous metallic synch.

Max had his sketchbook, while Karen had her cigarettes and something else she hadn't told Max about. They decided to wait on visiting the Peters Museum, preferring to explore the town to distract themselves, to burn off impending anxiety.

They stopped often for Max to sketch, Karen to smoke.

Dwayne gripped the steering wheel, nerves taut.

He had begun to consider the whole thing futile, like so many of his paranormal pursuits, but he had to keep trying. While theirs was hardly the clearest era on record, it was understood, perhaps more anecdotally than he was willing to admit, that the Agra tribe once here had seen things, had heard things, had made things beyond the limits of what mainstream society was willing to accept, let alone explain.

Every human mind was a puzzle piece of God. So went the teaching, a funny mixture of Hinduism and

Buddhism and pantheism and who knew what other of the millions of *-isms* flying around town. Every mind was a muscle of God, capable of God-like powers if flexed, if exercised, if honed, and, especially, if combined. What if we all shared in flexing such capabilities? What if we all shared a singular vision? Touchable, movable manifestation, maybe, and.... *Poof!* It's there.

So went the teaching.

Here, dreams had been known to come true. Here, the imagination was rumored to have flesh.

Memories of Jenny were his thousand passengers as Dwayne rumbled on toward the outskirts of town.

The boy led Ritter through the TwiFalls Inn's main entrance, past the lobby, and upstairs toward a stucco archway with tiled designs like those of a Mexican restaurant. The trek stopped at an airy lounge, its large windows like living murals of the town spread below, its furniture lit in the gray sunshine filtering through the glass.

A man in a raggedy t-shirt, shorts, and flip-flops sat sipping cola in an armchair. Between his long hair and beard, his head was an auburn shrub.

"Mr. Norman Ritter," said the boy, beaming, "it is my pleasure to introduce Bennett Wilson."

Ritter stuck out his hand.

Wilson stood, bowed quickly, then sat back down, leaving Ritter's hand unshaken.

"You're from Los Angeles?" Wilson asked after a mouthful of cola.

"I am. My name is Norman Ritter. I'm from *Direct Canvas* magazine."

"I know *Direct Canvas*," Wilson said. "You guys are growing, aren't you?"

"Guess you could say that, yeah. We started out pretty local but we're getting national distribution now." *All right, cut the stupid small talk.* "I was just over at Peters... admiring some of your work—"

"No, you weren't."

"Excuse me?"

"Were you really *admiring* my work?"

"Well... I...."

"Because admiration should be left to students and inferiors. You look skyward. Sometimes it swallows you and you just can't get over it. Everything just sucks. So you just start over... clean slate. That's what I'm doing."

"I don't think I follow—"

"Starting over—with art. I'm part of Neo-Naturalism because it's a whole blank page to start on. The things I learned my first three semesters of art school—out. Any 'anxiety of influence'—out. My old inhibitions—out. Blank page, man, I'm telling you."

"Tell me exactly how you see this Neo-Naturalist style. Avant-garde?"

"I suppose one could, but it's not. Avant-garde was a reaction, a way of breaking from the rut of portraits and landscapes and still-lifes. This isn't a statement or reaction. It just is. It's its own organism, part of the cycle. We've gone through our summers and falls and winters and are re-emerging once more into spring."

"I see."

"Like Feldman says, you should imagine art as a lost old man who can barely see, crazy with dementia. We're the ones to tap on his shoulder, and politely turn him around and in the right direction."

"Then what *is* the right direction?"

"I shouldn't be the one to tell you," Wilson said. "Wait for Feldman. Although, truth be told, I have no idea what Feldman is gonna talk about tonight. Magicians almost never reveal their secrets."

"Magician? You consider yourself a magician?"

"A magician is a creator. I consider myself a creator."

"That brings to mind," Ritter began, then cleared his throat and started over. "I have to ask... this whole Count thing of Feldman's. What's that all about?"

"Count thing?"

"Yeah, how he claims to be some Count from three hundred years ago."

"Oh." Wilson polished off his cola and crumpled the can. "Yeah, that. No one really knows if that's true or not. Of course, we all thought it was bull when we first heard about it, but you know...." Wilson scrambled for the next sentence.

Ritter tapped his pencil on the notepad as the boy stood, patient and waiting, with the same beaming bellhop smile, at his side.

"That guy knows everything, honestly," Wilson continued. "He's a walking and breathing encyclopedia, and he talks like a page of literature. He's been all over the place, seen so many things... it's almost hard to believe now that there isn't something strange about him."

"He's not just a world-class traveler?"

"He is, but he's someone who can get you to believe anything, I think. There's an authenticity about him. I mean, he described to me once how pleasantly surprised he was at King Louis XIII's hygiene, but that his handshake was slippery. It was so anecdotal, and so *true*."

"How did you meet him?"

"One of his showings up in Seattle. I was at art school and not loving it, and I actually skipped class to check it out. Went on from there."

"And your pieces...." Ritter paused, hands in mid-gesture like he was about to clap a passing insect. "Or your work—"

"I throw whatever I feel at them. Feldman has a good way of bringing that out of you."

"Bringing what out of you?"

"A Neo-Naturalist turns himself inside-out. He doesn't dress up his work, or encode it in metaphor, in cryptic treasure hunts. The art no longer passes through both hemispheres of the brain. It comes from the stomach, from the heart, from a time and a place even before language, certainly before our current civilization—splattered full and raw. The human soul needs no translator."

Ritter regarded him.

"The negative space of humanity," Wilson said, "is how Feldman refers to it. The stuff unseen and unspoken that completes us."

"That seems like expressionism."

"It *does* express," Wilson said. "It expresses a renewal."

Outside, the foliage wavered in the wind. *Growing cold. Colder.*

"You'll see."

Ritter began, "So, Mr. Wilson—"

"Who are you?" Wilson asked abruptly.

"Excuse me?"

"Who are you? Why are you sitting here with me?"

Ritter snorted. *These immature, dipshit artists.* They were comedians too. They could do anything, fuck with anyone. They loved it.

But Wilson continued staring expressionless at him.

"Mr. Wilson, I'm interviewing you for *Direct Canvas*. My name's Norman Ritter."

Across Wilson's face floated a look Ritter had seen just ten minutes ago, at the start of the interview.

"I know *Direct Canvas*," Wilson said. "You guys are growing, aren't you?"

III

The Peters Museum proved somehow bigger on the inside than on the outside. Probably an illusion fostered by all these milling people, Max figured. The place bustled hotly with conversation and thought and bodies, many of them esteemed—ostensibly—and older than he. He felt like the one penny in a wallet of bills.

Will any of these people recognize me? Unlikely.

Despite recent traction, his career still hung in limbo between the comforts of anonymity and the pressures of an Iconic Voice. But could any artist working today even *become* such a thing as an Iconic Voice? Especially a "fine artist"? It seemed impossible—today's ocean was too full, crashed too loudly. Everyone drowned.

For those few who might reach the sunlit shores, the fickle tide would snatch them back soon enough, return them to forgotten recesses.

Max checked his pockets, casually at first. Then, finding them empty, his hands frantically patted his front and back and cargo pockets. All empty.

He had only one other alternative.

"Karen...."

"What's wrong?" she asked.

"I don't have any packets."

"Packets?"

"Sauce packets, you know...."

"Oh."

"Could you lend me a stick?"

"What?"

"You have any on you?"

"You quit."

"This is an emergency. Please."

She grasped his arm and led him toward the entrance, narrowly avoiding collisions with several crisply-clad patrons.

The chilly dusk stood in stark contrast to the breath-body heat of the Peters.

They sat on the curb, feet planted in the street. A nearby lamppost threw harsh light against the evening. Karen equipped her mouth with a cigarette and lit up. Max watched with anticipation as she took a drag and flicked the ashes from the head, spewing them like fireflies into the dark.

She handed the cigarette to Max. "We share. Take a few puffs, but you're not getting a full one to yourself."

Max took it and dragged, smoke filling and possessing him like a mindless ashen spirit.

"You okay?" Karen asked.

"Probably not." He took another sip of smoke. "I don't know. It just all came rushing up to me, I guess, these past couple weeks — meeting you, taking a trip with a near stranger, and... this. I mean, this day has lived in my head for over twenty years, and suddenly it's just popped up. It's... weird. Can't describe it."

"It's lived in my head too, Max, but we're not even sure this Feldman guy is who we think he might be. We don't have much of anything to go on, really, except fuzzy photos and a vague-ish gut feeling."

"And my drawings."

An acknowledging silence.

"I'm not good with gut feelings," Max said. "I get a lot of them, and somehow I still can't handle them. And this crowd isn't helping things, either."

Karen took the cigarette from his fingers and dragged long.

"How can you stand it?" Max said.

"What?"

"This... all this. You seem to just take everything in stride, like it's a river and you've given up on trying to fight the current or something."

"Pretty useless to try and fight a river's current, I'd say, if you're talking about rough water."

"You know what I mean."

"I do. That's why I just said that." She finished off the cigarette, dropped it, and crushed it out. "You ready to go back inside? Grand entrance is any time now."

"Sure, I guess."

They returned to the show. Max overheard a conversation between a middle-aged woman and a younger man regarding a piece on parchment paper:

long silhouetted humanoids and animals sketched in crude, simplistic display.

"I just love the sparseness," said the woman. "It's a complex sparseness. It whittles the beauty of art to its core. See how much life these figures carry? A whole semester's worth of my freshmen gestures couldn't equal just one of these in their vibrancy. Quite remarkable, really."

"'Excuse me," Karen said, leaning into the woman's space.

"Yes?"

"Do either of you know when Feldman is supposed to come out and give his little speech?"

"I've no idea, actually," said the younger man. "I was wondering the same thing myself."

The timing of the inquiry was exquisite, as near the corner of the wing a man called out to the crowd, "Everyone, may I have your attention please?"

Bodies righted, heads turned, conversation dribbled off.

"My name is Jack McGrath," said the man, face sooted with beard. "I'm a curator here at the Peters Museum in Twilight Falls, and I'd like to thank you for attending this very special show. And as an extra treat for those of you who could join us tonight, I'd like to personally introduce the featured artists of this show, Roger Krauford, Bennett Wilson, and, of course, Clifford Feldman, who will be addressing you tonight with a few words about his work."

As the crowd began filing toward the small stage in the corner of the show floor, Max breathed fast and heavy. He noticed rapid breathing on Karen's part, too.

People congregated before the little stage, a little elevation where a silk-suited Feldman and two others—presumably the artists Krauford and Wilson—stood with smug eyes and smiles in their foot-high sophistication above everyone else in the room. It was startling, the contrast between Feldman's attire and that of the other two artists, like beach-goers backdropping a presidential address.

Feldman was shorter than Max had envisioned, and even looked different from the photograph Dwayne had showed him. Max thought with bewildered amusement how the man always seemed to change with each new version he saw. There was the *Moon Watch* painting, which differed from Dwayne's article photo, which differed now from the flesh and blood visage. Max crawled a sharp and focused eye over Feldman's features, the skin kneaded by age, the neat-slicked, silvery hair, the sunken eyes. Where was he in there? In Feldman, Max perceived nothing of himself.

'Do you want to?'

"Ladies and gentlemen," Feldman said, his voice booming command. "I'd like to thank you for coming tonight, for supporting the Peters Museum and its good people, as well as the good people of Twilight Falls. Surely, if we are to have another Renaissance, the Michelangelos and the Donatellos would find themselves here."

Murmurs slithered through the crowd.

Max saw Karen constantly shifting her weight from leg to leg, and biting her lip too.

"Art is a shadow cast by our dreams and desires," said Feldman, "and, in any form it takes, art has long been the platform for discussion of larger questions. Artists can't avoid it. Even if they intend no message or meaning, their engaging in creation, following their nature, *is* the meaning.

"Art has survived much madness and many mutations, not because of the artists, but because of the art, the thing itself. It is the God-act. Nature, an orphan, seeks a parent in us. But what have we done with our potential? We have drifted off-course toward a garish-colored Dark Age, where the art is smeared to dulling ubiquity, packaged and meaningless. Art is an embryonic glimpse of higher realms, a baby-step toward the Creation becoming the Creator. In distorted form, we knew this long ago, in ages when art was a tool of the divine, when its practitioners worshipped, patronized by ultimate powers of the land.

"Except we continued to use art to *touch* God, to reach *out* to Him, rather than finding Him pulsing in our very own veins. So we reached out and found no one, and thus fell disillusioned, and ravaged our minds with questions, drove our souls into the despairing frenzy of movement after movement, meaning after meaning.

"Where are we now? We've reached a precipice. Art has been stuffed and mounted, life-like but not real. We will go on repeating this despair without direction. I propose not. I propose we not lose ourselves in trivial repetition. For long enough, we have staggered blind. Fueled by questions, we have reached the cul-de-sac. But imagine the track we might have followed had we been given an answer at the outset. Some say this would have destroyed the asking, which is the momentum of all art and science. The beauty is the treasure hunt, they say. But what good is a treasure hunt without a treasure? Would you scour ad nauseum lands and fields and streams without some assurance of value, without at least a tip?

"To me, art has always had a clear spiritual purpose, one we knew but muddied, one we allowed slip from our most base understanding. That purpose is to put us on the path to Godhood, one creative work at a time. With such endeavors, we master a meta-reality, apprenticed for greater realms."

Karen reached into her pants and sweatshirt pockets, producing several sheets of folded-up papers. Max saw glimpses of fanciful colors and identified them instantly.

"You brought those?" he whispered.

"Yeah, just *shh*." Karen unfolded the papers and clutched them all in one hand as she fished through her back pants pocket, bringing out a pack of Nicorette gum.

"I knew this stuff was gonna come in handy," she said. She popped a gum in her mouth, chewed for a minute, then spit it into her hand and stuck it on the back of one of Max's old Lone Ranger drawings, which she proceeded to stick to the wall just behind her, making sure to slap it on tight and noisy.

At the thudding sound, Feldman quieted.

"What are you doing?" a woman asked.

"Just adding to the show," Karen said.

Max kept his distance.

"Young lady, what are you doing?" called a voice. McGrath.

Feldman's speech halted entirely. The room lost momentum.

Heads swiveled toward Max and Karen, facial spotlights glaring.

"Recognize the new addition, Mr. Feldman?" Karen called, staring directly at the artist as if he were now the only one in the room. She remained unfazed by the many stares.

Unlike Krauford and Wilson and everyone else Max could see, Clifford Feldman seemed intrigued by the antics.

"Who are you?" he asked.

Karen stood close by the drawings stuck to the wall. Her breath seemed labored, her face taut. Museum security pushed past the crowds toward her, like bloodhounds pursuing prey through a cornfield.

Feldman stopped them. "Who are you?" he asked again.

"You recognize these?" she said.

The man's grin never wavered, as if he anticipated a punch line.

"Ever live in Arondale, Mr. Feldman? Raise a family there? Ever leave your family there? Or how about Baltimore?"

"What a nice treat," Feldman said. "Karen Eisenlord, everybody!"

Feldman scanned the audience, registering every head, every pair of eyes, and found Max.

Max's stomach sank.

"And... Max Higgins." Feldman seemed more wistful at recognizing him.

Goddammit Karen why did you do this to me?

"Ladies and gentlemen, it seems two unexpected guests have emerged from my past to celebrate this show, as well." Feldman gestured toward both Karen and Max. "My son and my daughter. Two of many."

"What?" Karen called.

Feldman spoke over a bubbling pond of conversation. "When it comes to my work, I have no regrets."

Karen was silent... breathing... breathing hard.

"We seek the creative force throbbing beneath our consciousness," said Feldman. "That ultimate and effortless maker of things. We are all fruits of it, as are you. Does that not make you the ultimate artwork? And Max?"

Karen slumped toward the floor and began to cry. Museum officials approached and took her by the arms, and led her to the exit. Her crying trickled into darkness.

All heads then centered on Max. Through the constellations of eyes, he saw the man from L.A., the journalist, the *Direct Canvas* guy — Reitman, no Ritter — Norman Ritter — his expression as shocked and confused as the many around him.

'We didn't have a dad, Max. We had a father.'

He ran toward the exit, nearly knocking over two people. The door clanged open and wide, hit its limit, then slammed shut, sealing the show in prickly silence.

Karen knelt on the grass by the parking lot. She had taken the band from her hair and unclasped her ponytail.

Max took slower and slower steps the closer he got to her. "Karen, look, I'm sorry I — "

"Max, shut up, don't worry about it." She sniffled. Tears had fallen down her face, and now hung on the edge of her chin. "We just go down in different ways. You want to crawl into a hole and die, and I want to go out in a blaze of glory... although I don't think 'glory' would be the right term."

Crawl into a hole and die?

"I just didn't — "

"I said shut up and don't worry about it." She wiped at the tears.

In dejected silence they sat on the museum's damp front lawn. Max picked at grass while Karen lit a cigarette. She inhaled hard and fast and the smoke returned in spastic shuddering coughs.

"You okay?" Max asked.

Slapping her chest, she said, "I'm okay."

Suddenly the museum door opened behind them. They turned to see a formidable silhouette, drawn quickly into light.

Clifford Feldman approached them.

"The fuck does he want?" Karen muttered.

A laundry-cycle of nausea churned in Max's gut.

"Karen Eisenlord," Feldman said. "Max Higgins."

Can't get enough of the names? Say them one more time say them —

"I recognize your anger and agitation," Feldman said. "But you should know — my loyalty is only to the demands of the flesh, and the spirit. Many of you exist. Only the fittest will survive, however. And the fittest find one another. Like you two."

They looked at one another. Karen looked at Feldman but Max still wrestled with his stomach and couldn't yet look at him.

"Come with me," Feldman said. "I want to show you both something."

"Why?" Karen said. "Why should we come with you?"

"Because you will. Otherwise your journey here, the very finding of yourselves and me, will have been in vain."

IV

Max was ever envious of Feldman's power, gravitas, whatever the hell to call it — a power harnessed only from a monolithic certainty in one's worldview. Unjustified, always, effective though it was in the swaying of softer, more accommodating minds, like right now, as Feldman ushered them across the parking lot toward a white limousine. A chauffeur stood by the door, popping it open as they approached.

"Watch your head, sir," said the driver woodenly.

Max reluctantly climbed in, and Karen followed.

Feldman slid inside and closed the door behind him. He took a seat across from Karen and Max, that wide grin still printed across his face.

The limousine purred to life.

"Where are we going?" Karen asked.

"To my own gallery," said Feldman. "To the other show that I want you both to see."

Max wanted to speak, but couldn't sneak a word past his queasiness. He pointed to an empty glass.

"What would you like, Max?"

"Water."

"Ice?"

He nodded, and Feldman expediently fixed him the drink.

The limo moved steadily through Twilight Falls, past the darkening downtown shops and cafés and the perfect right-angled residential blocks and the northeastern section not seen earlier, the houses of which appeared shuttered and rickety, and from whose windows Max imagined ghosts might forever peer somber upon the streets.

"Let me ask you both something," Feldman said, pouring himself a scotch, neat. "Are you passionate?"

Karen glanced at Max, who couldn't control his hands shaking. *Focus on the water. The water. The water.*

"What does that mean? Passionate?" Karen said.

"Just that. Do you have passion? For anything you do. And regardless of your reply, I'll know the truth."

"Then you can answer for us."

"Sure." Feldman took sip of scotch and leaned forward. The limo, edging past the fringes of town, made a right turn up a steep incline. "But first I want to ask you another question."

They waited.

"Both of your mothers—they were quite religious, weren't they?"

"You could say that."

"Yours, Max?"

"Yes."

"I often spread my seed through the religious ones," Feldman said. "Christians, correct?"

Karen closed her eyes, nodded.

"That was by design. I detest religion, but for artists, such an environment does generally make for a grand Darwinian trial. It tests true passion. I imagine both of you were restrained, hampered in some way by the beliefs of your mothers. Yet you both found the impassioned calling of your art and your ideas too strong to be sedated, censored, or abolished."

"I'm not an artist," Karen said. "You and Max are the only artists here."

Feldman smiled. "I disagree, as would any tribesman of the Agras."

Karen stirred.

"You've heard of them."

"Briefly. Recently."

"Historical records put them in this area. There's the back and forth about what they were, who they were, even if they truly existed, but long-standing throughout the debate is wisdom by which all can abide, by which I abide every day. Namely, that together, we are all God, broken up, dusted across the universe. What greater aspiration can an artist have to achieve? In fact, it negates the achievement because one is already *there*. From this realization on, it's a matter of experiential reveling. Pure creating... creation."

They didn't respond.

"Karen," said Feldman. "What do you do?"

"I spank people for a living."

Feldman blinked. "Come again?"

"I work at a fetish club—whips and chains and the whole nine yards."

Feldman raised his hands in mock celebration, and that damn smile never waned. "Of course you're an artist. You're what the Agras might have termed a 'destroyer.' Do you know what I'm talking about?"

"No."

"The Agras believed everything created comes about through a creator, a destroyer, a collector, and a teacher. All roles are rather self-explanatory. All are sculptors of reality, tools in the crafting of this world, on mental and material levels.

"You destroy people, Karen," Feldman went on. "That's your art. And you know as well as any they want to be destroyed, no matter how wrong they think it is. They *want* you to tear them down, undress them of civilization, put in their veins that primal pleasure. Max may build, but you... you demolish. Such things are really cosmically conjoined twins." He took a long sip of the scotch, keeping his eyes on them. "Little wonder as to the why, or how, of you two finding one another."

Max looked outside, at the night striped with imposing, Titan-bodied trees. They'd passed into the redwoods.

He looked back. The town was no longer visible.

V

James awoke to nothing.

What dream? No dream, none that had left marks. Beyond the sliding glass door of James Cannon's bedroom, Sherman Canal rippled on, pebbled by moonlight, the dark feathery shapes of mallards cruising the surface. He sat up and rubbed his face. This marked the third time this week he'd awakened in the middle of the night. He hadn't been able to get back to sleep the first time.

His mother had told him as a child he'd had night terrors. "Blood-curdling screams," she had said. "Sent us racing to you where you'd be sitting up and shaking, face all pale." Pops the Judge, all sour, summoned from bed. What was wrong? Nothing. The nightmares had made a clean getaway, some kind of hit-and-run on the psyche.

In nothing but his plaid boxers, James rose and stood by the sliding glass door. He watched the darkened houses across the canal. Maybe his inability to recall his dreams accounted for his lack as an artist. Maybe the gods deemed him a vessel unfit for Vision, his arms hardly long enough to touch hands in embracing whatever fat, wide truth smothered everyone.

What the hell am I thinking about?

Penelope. I should be thinking about Penelope. Or Teresa.

After turning on the bedside lamp, he pulled open the bottom nightstand drawer and retrieved an old sketchpad, creased and yellowed. Graphite memories of youth hummed past his eyes, visions he thought might be Visions, whatever that meant.

Toward the middle of the sketchpad he found a slew of animal drawings from an Anthropomorphic Drawing class he'd taken five or so years back at Santa Monica City College—leopards, elephants, apes.

Lame. Terribly lame.

He found unused pages, then retrieved a pencil.

Penelope. Penelope. So hopelessly intoxicating. What is it about her?

Los Angeles crawled with gorgeous women, brought here from all over by daydreams of The Biz. In any objective sense, Penelope was, by L.A. standards, a good seven, maybe seven-point-five, head-turning but not *too* spectacular. So what was it? All the clichés, he supposed. The Spunk; that she gave him things no one else in the world gave him. More, that she knew things about him known by no one else in the world. And yeah, she was sexy, any way sliced.

He thought about their last session, Penelope bound by her wrists in the middle of the room, her arms stretched up and splayed, her nicely-curved figure so vulnerable—there for the taking. He'd approached her from behind, slid his arms around her waist, tickled her belly. She'd flinched but he held her firmly in place, his breath inches from her face.

Didn't expect that, did you?

'No,' she'd said. '*I didn't.*'

James imagined her spanking a bound duplicate of herself as hundreds of other twin spectators watched and breathed and hardened, moistening beneath their garments. Or maybe they were all naked to begin with—yes, thousands of her supple, college-aged breasts filling his mind, filling him. And they all wore their hair in ponytails, tied back with her classic velvet scrunchie. James loved that scrunchie—it gave her a kind of girly juvenile charm. Each time they had a session, if she didn't have it on, he would request it.

He began drawing. *More lameness.* How did that clerk at the Sirens Shop do it? The guy ran about the page as if it were an amusement park for his hand, bounding and dancing and singing his subjects to life, into another life. Effortless, but of course, that guy—Nick? Matt?—was a professional artist; couldn't just sprint to his level.

The guy knew Penelope, too, it seemed. That would be the best way. Go through him. Set up an art show, invite him, and maybe Penelope would come. How would that work, though? Would she feel embarrassed seeing him? He knew the Penelope schtick was an act, but she would have to treat him in a normal fashion if they were to bump into one another somewhere. Then he could win her over, maybe... have her all to himself. She liked him, James could tell.

He'd begun with a gesture-sketch, the light impression of a humanoid, the foundation on which he'd place all the flesh and hair and features. It would be a wooden and lame Penelope, the Vision crumbling on its descent from mind to page, yet a Penelope nonetheless, a Penelope as he'd never seen her: naked; nice S-shaped curve of hair at the crotch; belly ring, which she had; hard, dark nipples.

Has she ever fucked someone in a session?

Despite no evidence one way or another, he was struck by sudden assurance that she must have.

'Teresa knows you're thinking about her. The stale lovemaking – it's obvious, right? Bored bored bored. Better destroy this drawing before she finds it.'

As if on cue, his phone rang. It was Teresa, crying, quiet voice.

"What's wrong?" he said.

"James...."

"What is it?"

"Dad died," she murmured. "Just a little while ago."

The limo slid methodically to a stop before a clearing, a puncture in the dense woods. An eerie feeling spread through Max that they'd entered a kind of inverse dimension, a place where legends had skin, uttered amongst themselves their own myths of towering cities, flying machines, and the strange, hairless apes that made them.

"We're here," said Feldman. He loosened his tie, unbuttoned his cuffs, then began unbuttoning his shirt.

What is he doing?

Karen looked out the window. "There are people out there."

Now shirtless and shoeless, Feldman climbed from the car and motioned them out. The limo driver remained in his seat, reading a newspaper.

"Come on," Feldman said. "It's all right."

Max glanced at Karen and Karen glanced at him, sharing a tight, unspoken promise to stick by one another. Slowly, they maneuvered out of the limousine just as Feldman unbuckled his belt, his pants falling like a demolished building.

The air had cold sharp teeth. Nocturnal woodland noises pulsed in humming, buzzing percussion. Moonlight split into tiny slivers by the grand high canopy.

Max looked about, toward the clearing where the moon shone down unimpeded. The limo's headlights still burned, twin suns on the redwood trunks. With enough illumination, Max's eyes needed no adjustment to the scene before him—though the rest of him, he imagined, would now need far longer to adjust.

Scattered throughout the trees and the clearing were about twenty people, most bare naked, some adorned in clinging threads of a shirt or underwear. One man had on only a watch, another the last of a sock on his right foot. All stared at Max and Karen as they climbed from the vehicle. Some fixated; others went back to their individual business: picking at blades of grass, banging rocks, gnawing on a hunk of meat that looked like a squirrel, the result of a smoked-out campfire in the clearing. In hefty voices, some spoke words, or things resembling words. Their eyes were hollow of concern, white drops of wild clarity.

"What... is this?" Karen said.

"They're re-experiencing the world, these people," Feldman said. "Refreshed to a base—awe, terror, joy, love—a base on which to build a new human mode, a new construct of understanding, and approach to how we inherit our unique position. They're a second draft, if you will—brushstrokes of a collective masterpiece. What is currently left for us? Adding to failure. We're rerouting back to the start, to begin art, to begin *consciousness*, again."

Feldman pointed to one of the fully nude men, sitting on a rock and watching a large moth with something like curious excitement, loopy smiles. Childhood exhumed in his face.

"Robert Campbell," Feldman said. "Four kids, two-story house on Keller Avenue, and a financial consultant since he was twenty-nine. The world needs now only a moth to enthrall him."

One of the men approached a bare-chested woman and palmed one of her breasts. She yelped and struck him on the shoulder, trotted away, and he followed, grin unbroken. She laughed. Eyes so dazed, so unplugged, so....

...not here.

Like a hungry cat to the can opener, Feldman hurried back to the limousine and leaned in.

Max fought heightening nausea. *I'm at a zoo.* He closed his eyes. *I'm at a goddamn zoo. Gonna feed us to them. Stop. Fucking ridiculous.* But then, what *wasn't* ridiculous? What had happened? He had seen something never meant to be seen: God's egregious typo.

He moved in close to Karen, and rasped, "We need to get out of here."

She batted away a mosquito. "Where? How?"

Feldman returned, holding carefully a long thin vial filled with liquid. "There's a species of large climbing vine in the jungles of the Amazon and the Orinoco basins—*Banisteriopsis caapi* is the botanical name for it. When the vine's bark is boiled, it produces this." He indicated the vial. "Yaje, or Ayahuasca, juice. Once ingested, it opens realms long closed to us, exhibits for us the remarkable vastness and utter strangeness of this place we share. It makes of one an ancient human ancestor, small and wondering and humbled. It turns the stars back into heavens, puts minds back into pebbles and peaks. I found my meaning in it. The elder in me, the elder in all of us, emerged and spoke to me."

Max and Karen glanced at one another.

"He is our Grandfather." Feldman outstretched the vial. "Would you like a taste?"

"No," Karen snapped. "We want to go back. Now."

Feldman regarded them, the physical weight of his gaze moving back and forth. Distantly, he seemed almost disappointed.

Fuck you fuck you.

"This is a cyclical process," said Feldman. "It is ineluctable. Either we seek to renew, or nature will do so for us. An indivisible entity cannot defy itself."

The man looked at the vial, then peered wistfully up at the towering redwoods. He looked disappointed, and for a fleeting second Max almost felt ashamed.

Feldman dropped his gaze. "Shane can take you back into town, if you wish not to stay."

"Who's Sh—?"

"The driver."

Both Max and Karen hurried past Feldman and climbed into the limousine, the weight of the man's gaze hardly lifting.

Don't look back, Max thought. *Don't fucking look back.*

After a brief exchange with Feldman, Shane the driver started the engine and pulled away, back toward the road.

Don't look back!

Long moments of purring silence ensued, the tall straight cavern of the woods close and suffocating.

"This is my first time in a limo," Karen said.

"Mine too."

Suddenly she rose from her seat, scrounged about the miniature bar, and opened the fridge, where arrayed on the shelves were more vials of the liquid.

"What are you doing?" Max said.

"Taking a souvenir," she said, swiping one of the vials and shutting the fridge. "I don't know what we can do, but maybe we can get this stuff tested."

Max threw a glance at the dark shrub of Shane's head. "He can't hear us, right?"

Upon stopping at the Peters, Shane climbed out to open the door for them.

Hastily, Max got out first, waving him back. "We can get it," he said.

They exited, the vial clutched within Karen's baggy sweatshirt, then watched as the limo slunk back onto the dark-slick roads and vanished around a bend.

The Peters Museum now sat shuttered and empty, and neither Dwayne nor his van were anywhere in sight.

"Guess we can just wait for him to get back," Karen said, sitting down on the grass. "Dammit."

"There's no way to contact him?" Max sat beside her.

"Not really. I don't think he has a car phone. If he does, I don't know the number. But if he's going to look for us, it'll be here."

After a short, wind-whispering pause, Max said, "I think I could use a drink."

"No shit."

"Mind if I get a smoke?"

Without hesitation, Karen unloaded two cigarettes, handed one to Max, and lit them both.

"Did that even really happen?" Max said.

Karen blew out smoke, intermingled with a sigh.

They peered at the section of town around them until Max looked up. The clouds were parting, unveiling a sharp and infinite night, dotted with constellations, those cave-pictures painted by the eye. Art thrust outward at the cosmos. He identified Orion, watched other stars wink on as the clouds continued their cold, quiet rupture. Then he brought his head down and dragged on his cigarette.

"Humans," she had said. "They'll come around."

Dwayne sat atop the van, encompassed by the dark, moon-kissed tree line, and listened once again to her silent voice. Even before everything that had happened, Jenny's relaxed assurance, her good faith and unshakable niceness, had sometimes bothered him. Now it enraged him.

Not far away, the waterfalls hummed endlessly on, crickets and other insects a needling ruckus in the shadows of the underbrush. Even with civilization a mile or two away, there was forever something cleansing about being enveloped in woods. Suddenly, fairy tales were real again... or at least felt real. It was easy to deny the presence of the fantastical, even magical, when fed the world through pages or screens, when insulated by click-on comforts—where science somehow made the most sense; where God somehow made the most sense.

Yet out here, soaked in nature's cool purity, neither science nor God made the most sense. Dwayne knew, rather, a curious conjoining of the two. Intuition said the essence, the life force, was real. Who was he to argue?

Eyes closed. Breathing measured. See her. Feel her. Embrace her. She's there. Living at the corner of your eye, sheltered from the angry swarm of your doubts, fears, opinions.

'What do you think is going to happen, exactly? That she'll come strolling from the woods, radiant, tell of her long amazing detour but that she's back now and for good? Okay. Okay.'

Soft wet clouds drifted in, muddling the moon into ghostlight. The air grew colder, and Dwayne shivered.

Mind over matter. Warmth warmth I'm warm think of her and only her. Can't do this. Can't.

Fucking kid had wanted her. Obsessed. She had lain there under him, struggling and coughing and weakening beneath the press of the kid's hands on her throat.

The evil jackass had not gotten far; Dwayne had made sure of that.

How much of herself did Jenny lose in those seconds of final realization? How much of the person he loved had persisted to the last, lonely synapse in her dying brain?

Dwayne climbed down from the roof of the van and returned to the driver's seat, where he inhaled a shuddering breath. This would be the last time trying any of this shit. The stories of Twilight Falls were just that: stories. He had to stop putting hope in them.

But why couldn't he just move on, stop having faith in nonsense? Because, he supposed, it was the wordless assurance of this place that it wasn't nonsense. How the gut so easily trumped the head baffled him, but it did. What was he to do, shed everything he knew? How? Clear the rain leaves from the gutter.

Physically, humankind had long ago learned to walk erect. How much longer before its spirit could, as well?

"You'll come around," she'd said.

The scattered town lights lay ahead, framed in the silhouettes of walnut trees. The van curved down the road. Dwayne sat pensive inside. Did he have to get them? The urge to continue driving, to drive off, made a strong case in his bones.

You're Nemo on wheels, he realized. *Retired from it all, explorer of the darker, unseen realms. How utterly grand.*

The roads splayed into avenues, and Dwayne slowed his speed, the van rolling beneath orange sodium streetlights. Soon he arrived at the Peters Museum, in front of which sat two figures under a cloud of smoke.

When he pulled to the curb, both figures rose, brushed themselves off, and without a word climbed into the van.

"Howdy," Dwayne said. "How did everything go?"

"Let's just drive," said Max. "Get out of here."

Dwayne frowned. "That bad? You saw Feldman?"

Karen held out a vial. "Look at this. You know what it is?"

Dwayne delicately took the vial from Karen, turned on the van's interior light, popped off the lid, and smelled it.

"Looks like some watery solution... or salt water. What is this supposed to be?"

Karen glanced back at Max. "Clifford Feldman calls it Yaje."

"What? The Amazon drug?"

"I guess so. You know it, then?"

He nodded. "Uh-huh. Professor contact of mine at Tulane University tried it on a trip to South America, brought a sample back. For some tribes down there, it's a very sacred thing, used in shamanic rites of passage."

"Is it illegal?"

"Probably."

"Well, can we find out?" Karen said. "Can we take this somewhere and tell someone that people are taking it and destroying their fucking minds?"

Dwayne blinked twice. He dipped a finger into the vial, brought it to his tongue. "I don't think so."

"Why?"

"Because this is salt water."

Karen stared blank at him.

"Yeah, apparently, Yaje is pretty pungent. They put sweeteners in it down there, actually." Dwayne brought the vial to his lips and sipped.

Max and Karen studied him.

"Just salt water," he said. "Good for a canker sore."

Laughing and crying, James thought. What was their evolutionary purpose? Common wisdom said they enriched life, made worthwhile the blood-grind of survival. Yet who had dictated under what circumstance to use which? Society told us to cry at the dead. Why, then, did James consistently feel the urge to laugh at funerals? Crossed wires?

Then again, in the oppressive throes of mourning, all enjoyed the release of a chuckle. Why not more than a chuckle, then? Humans laughed at absurdity, and what greater absurdity could there be than having decades of sights, smells, sounds, touches, tastes, and thoughts flicked off like a light-switch? The soul's candle-flame, flickering precariously between nature's twitchy thumb and forefinger.

Keep it straight.

James perused the eulogy. The speech wasn't great—only a few line-edits beyond a first draft. Teresa might get mad, but she wouldn't know. He'd promised he'd give one, even though he felt disingenuous doing it.

He studied every face filing into the room: old; dumb-eyed, kids with no attention span; more old people. They'd be forgetful, perhaps. Nothing he said would stay with any of these people.

Through all the movement, all the talk and all the thoughts, Thomas Locke, Teresa's father, lay peacefully gray in the open casket.

One of Locke's old business associates, an Abe Worswick, gave James a firm handshake as he shook his head. "James," said Worswick. "You're the artist?"

James blinked. "I suppose. I'm an attorney."

"Oh," said the old man. "I remember Tom mentioning your shared love of art. He said something about opening a gallery with you. Whatever happened with that?"

James grinned, wide as the event would allow. "You'll find out soon enough, actually."

In good time, all took their seats, and a Reverend Mathis made opening remarks. He discussed Thomas Locke and his life and his legacy — the usual, plus Him. God this, God that.

James sat glazed. At one point, Teresa slid her lithe hand into his and he held it.

"...we will now hear from Mr. James Cannon, dear friend of Mr. Locke."

James approached the podium, buttoning his suit. He thanked Mathis, and felt the blood drain, tingling, from his face. He looked at the papers before him, coughed, then began.

"I know the pain of meeting the parents," he said. "I know it's kind of a cultural staple, this 'meeting the parents' of a significant other — the clammy hands, the stare-down, the interrogation. I've been shaken to my core in my day, and to put that in perspective, I'm a lawyer."

Chuckling.

James shook his head. "But there was none of that with Tom. We shared a lot. First time we met, I think my girlfriend Teresa, his lovely daughter —" He gestured. " — was jealous of how long we spoke. A big handshake and a big heart, those were the two things instantly recognizable about him.

"Many of you who knew Tom, I'm sure, are aware that, in addition to being a shrewd businessman, he was also a sucker for the arts. He and I shared that passion, and although it never came to fruition while he was alive, Tom and I often talked about working together to put up our own gallery here in Los Angeles. And today, I'm proud to announce that, with Tom's generous bequest, I will be opening the Cannon-Locke Gallery in Venice, and hope to have it open in the summer."

An approving murmur ran through the crowd. In the rustling flowerbed of discussion bloomed nice little adjectives like "honorable" and "wonderful" and "great" and—and what else were they saying? What else?

He met eyes with Teresa. Between the tear streaks on her face, a proud smile broke.

MIKE ROBINSON

Chapter 6

I

"So one strawberry says to another, if you hadn't been so fresh last night, we wouldn't be in this jam today!"

Southwest was telling jokes again, at least this pilot was, and the effort brightened Ritter. It was a family-friendly joke, a joke with combed hair and a wide 1950s smile. Wholesome.

Not like the world going haywire below him.

I gotta become a real writer. Whatever the hell that means.

Ritter noticed his neighbor, a man with a bushy mustache, shaking his head and chuckling.

"My friend was on a Southwest flight one time," said the neighbor, "where the pilot told a joke that probably got him fired."

"Oh yeah?"

"The captain asked the co-pilot if he blew bubbles when he was a kid. The co-pilot said yes, and the captain said that he'd seen him that morning, and that he said hi."

"Wait, what?"

"Bubbles. He said that he'd seen Bubbles. You don't get it?"

"Oh, that he blew a guy named Bubbles." This time Ritter shook his head. "Har har."

"Best part was the static shock it sent through the plane. You could feel it." The man advanced a callused hand. "I'm Walt, by the way."

"Norm."

They shook hands. Ritter noticed a butterfly tattoo on the back of Walt's hand.

"Should I leave you alone during this flight?" Walt asked.

"Why? Do I look like I want to be left alone?"

Walt made a *mas-o-menos* gesture. "Borderline, I'd say. You look like you got something on your mind."

"I'm definitely a little disoriented after this trip. I was in Twilight Falls for an art exhibition, a rather strange one, too."

"You an artist?"

"No. More a critic, journalist. I write for an art magazine in Los Angeles. *Direct Canvas*?" Ritter produced his business card.

Walt studied it wistfully. "Sounds like one hell of a review's in store."

In the back of his mind, Ritter thought about Max Higgins and the girl who had come to see him. They had interrupted the show. Had it been an act contrived by Feldman? Who knew. Maybe he ought to contact Max when he got back, see if there was some sense to be made of the parallel universe glimpsed in Twilight Falls that was edging into his own.

"You be careful with that arsenal you got," Walt said randomly.

Ritter raised an eyebrow. "Arsenal?"

"Yeah. The English language. With one little stab or pinch of a nicely-sharpened word, you can kill things. Or, even worse, make them immortal."

"I want to illuminate," Ritter said. "Instruct. Inspire."

"Without being in a classroom, I take it?"

"Well, what if the *city* is my classroom?"

Walt chuckled. Down the aisle, flight attendants brought drinks and pretzels and wide fixed smiles. Walt popped open his bag of pretzels and crammed them past his salt-and-pepper mustache.

Bong. The captain came on. Descent toward Los Angeles had begun. And, "Have you heard the one about the grape and the raisin?"

They drove for many silent miles and hours, winding southbound down Highway 1. For the first time since the demoralizing start of his freshman year at Rheta, Max felt no urge to draw. It didn't bother him, though this indifference did.

"Listen, I think we all could use a little loosener," Dwayne said. "Little time to thaw out."

Karen frowned. "What does that mean?"

"Max, check the cooler. I think I got a bottle of Jack in there, if you'd be so kind as to fetch it. A stretch and a swig. How about it?"

"You're driving, Dwayne," Max said, hesitating at the cooler.

"Relax, Maximo," he said. The nickname had resumed its brisk playfulness, but still felt forced. "I won't take much. Plus I have a higher tolerance than the two of you put together, and I'll walk off any drops of the stuff before I hit the wheel again."

"Sounds like a challenge," said Karen. "You think it's just my lungs that get all the abuse?"

Max opened the cooler: the infamous package of special cookies; crackers; chips; sandwich with a Europe-shaped spot of mold on the bread; and the single vial of salt water Karen had snatched from the limousine.

"Where's the bottle?" Max asked.

"On the bottom. Just lift the other stuff."

"Got it." He handed it up front to Karen.

They arrived again in the vicinity of Big Sur. Dwayne pulled over to the side of the road at a clearing spread before a wall of pines printed flat and black against the sky. The threesome piled out, huddled in a small loose circle. Above them, the white pupil of the moon stared over the tree line and rendered in funereal light their tired features.

Karen took a swig of the bottle and passed it to Max, who hesitated, then shut his eyes and sipped—second taste of alcohol in his entire life. *Bitter, acrid, tingling, but perversely enjoyable.* He relayed the bottle to Dwayne.

"I'm sorry I wasn't with you guys," said Dwayne. "At the museum, I mean."

"It's fine," said Max. "I'm sorry I *was* there."

"It's just... every time I go to that town I go in with a different intention, but I always end up doing the same thing. I tell myself I'm going to see this, or do this, but I get pulled in the same direction and I don't ever do anything else, like the place is afraid of me sniffing and scoping it out so it tosses a steak at me like I'm some guard dog. Some distraction tactic, and I fall for it every fucking time."

Max and Karen glanced at one another.

"What do you do?" Max asked.

"I lost someone, too," Dwayne said. "My fiancée."

"Oh," Karen said. "I'm sorry."

"I know this is going to sound nuts, but remember what I said before, when we came to town? That there was some kind of extra concentration of artistic energy there?"

Both nodded, slowly.

"There's a little more to it, or at least some people claim there's more to it. Legend says the *stain* of the Agra tribe is still there, that they opened some kind of other realm, or did something, that bled otherworldly power into Twilight Falls. It's a realm one can usually access only through a lifetime of spiritual practice, like meditation. The paint of the gods, as one writer put it. But going there is like a shortcut to enlightenment, to the god-stuff that supposedly translates thought into reality, manifests dreams.

"Sounds like a cheesy *Twilight Zone* plot, I know. In fact, I think it was, sort of, but I can't help it. I've tried to bring her back so many times, and I've failed just as many times, but I keep going back. I keep thinking: this time I've gotten it down. Gotten what down? Why am I blinded with the possibility of this shit? I mean, I know why, but you'd think by now I'd get better at controlling the Santa Claus impulse. Left over from childhood, maybe."

Karen wondered if Clifford Feldman knew of these stories, and an eerie thought came to her that of *course* he did, that that was precisely the aim of this deluded "renewal" agenda: that somehow a bunch of people, their minds wiped clear of the old world, would sit around and, under his twisted tutelage, equipped with this "power," engender a new one, dream it pulsing into reality.

So they thought.

As if reading her thoughts, Dwayne said, "I'm sure Feldman's into the whole Agra thing. It seems to attract a lot of artists, a lot of men, too. Want to know truly what I think? I think men are massively envious of women being able to make babies. We loan the ingredients, but they brew it up and put it out. It's living art. Men desperately want to make living art, too, to make something that will last and endure, affirm their existence. It's why I think there are more major male artists than women artists. It's not just patriarchy. It's terrible insecurity. Women are more... of the continuum. Men scramble to find meaning, lusting and battling and creating for it. Shakespeare and Hitler are embers of the same firestorm."

Max thought about his business card-sized prints of all his canvases, safe and pocketed, signs and reminders of his work, his existence, his babies — preserved, there in case. *In case of... well... what?*

For several seconds, the birds and the insects sang to the darkness. Then Karen said, "Feldman told me I was a destroyer."

Dwayne studied her.

Max's head hung. Had that whole episode with Feldman in the woods even happened? Sometime, just prior to it, the harder touch of reality had fallen away; they had stumbled over a precipice into some recess of the weird, where sensations unintended, unreal, unfit for typical human veins had filled them, suspended them in a dream-stasis until they reached once more the other side of the regular world.

Karen rose and dusted off the rear of her jeans. "I need to pee," she said, then made her way into the shadows.

Max kept an eye on her as she cautiously made her way into the brush, crackling branches and leaves. By now, the Jack bottle had made its rounds three or four times over, and with his low tolerance the alcohol had already submerged him. The drink seeped and spread, crashed and rolled and trickled and streamed, leaving no rock unturned and filling emotional tiger traps, pits into which he would often fall but through which he could now simply float.

"How many brain cells am I killing?" Max said.

"What?" Dwayne said.

"Is it a ruthless slaughter up there? How come you're not drunk?"

"Oh, I'm feeling it, but as I said, I can hold my own. And stop fucking around, Maximo, you've only had like three or four gulps. You're not full-on drunk yet. Or then, maybe you are. When was the last time you drank?"

"Something like college."

"Been a while then."

Max nodded. He scratched his right forearm, scattered bug bites.

"You're a little loose," Dwayne said. "Maybe this is the best time to tell you."

"Tell me what?"

Dwayne hesitated, glanced toward where Karen crunched in the woods, listened to a faint trickling sound.

"You're an artist, Max," he said, lowering his voice. "You know it really only brings in pennies and dimes. The starving artist stereotype is probably the truest of all stereotypes."

Max snorted.

"Well, you honestly think I could make a living, driving around as I do, off art?" Dwayne gave a wheezy laugh. "That's really not what I do."

"Oh yeah?" Max said, taking the bottle from Dwayne and tossing back another shot.

"I'm a private investigator," Dwayne said. "Private eye, gumshoe, whatever. Humphrey Bogart had a bunch of names for it in those old movies."

"Huh?"

"Karen hired me... to watch you. She knew there was someone out there, that she had a half-sibling, because her mother had found evidence of her father's correspondence with what looked like another family in California. The mother knew there was funny business going on but never told the father, I guess, or Karen, for that matter. Karen just found out on her own over the years."

Anxiety tried to bite at Max's stomach but the Jack had dulled its teeth. Besides, even beyond the booze, there was something right about what Dwayne had just told him. A mental Tetris block had fallen into place.

"So how long have you been following me?" Max said. "And why wasn't it you who went to see Norman Ritter?"

"That was her choice. I'd been on your tail for only a week or so, and kind of loosely at that point. I think Karen wanted to establish herself here, plant her feet before going out to look for you. Plus, I'm sure she needed to save up for my services, but I cut my daily rate for her."

"How nice."

Dwayne shrugged. "She reminds me of myself."

Max sat quietly as Karen emerged from the darkness and strode toward the van.

"Think I left my cigarettes in the car," she muttered.

"We should probably get going soon," Dwayne said, pushing himself up.

Max said, "I should probably care a lot more than I do right now."

Dwayne looked at him.

"Probably the alcohol talking," Max continued. "I don't know, I do care, but really, after this ridiculous weekend it's a nice little cherry on top... and it's not even really a cherry, I'd say. It makes sense. Yeah, that's it. It's the only thing that's made sense this week."

"Okay," Dwayne said. "I was feeling weirder with you not knowing."

"Funny... seems like that would be Karen's job."

Dwayne leaned in closer to Max. "Well, that girl's got good bark. I'm sure she's into the what-you-don't-know-won't-hurt-you theory, but I think she was also just afraid of losing you before knowing you. Maybe."

Dwayne started for the car while Max remained on the ground, salvaging whole parts of thought from the liquor.

"So what am I supposed to do?" Max said with a faint smirk. "Act all betrayed? Throw a tantrum? Would that be the normal way to respond?"

"All up to you, Maximo," said Dwayne, turning slightly toward him. "Anarchy for everyone is only an excuse away."

II

Around two-thirty Sunday morning, the lights of Los Angeles rose up in the windshield, lambent acne on the dark face of the hills. For simplicity's sake, Max told Dwayne he could drop him off at the Sirens Shop, only a mile or two from Karen's apartment in eastern Santa Monica.

After a hug from Karen and a shake from Dwayne, Max stepped out of the van and crawled back into his nightly hole.

His co-worker Tyler, covering for him that night, sat slouched at a personal computer just behind the counter, clicking away at boxes and graphics on the bright humming screen. With every command, the machine croaked and groaned.

"Wow," said Max. "Jerry finally got the computer going."

"Yeah, he finally came through," said Tyler. "How's your trip? You back already?"

"No, you're hallucinating again."

"Thanks." Tyler had not pulled his eyes from the screen. "You should be nice to me. I worked the day shift, too, and now I'm here covering your vacationing ass."

"Trust me, it wasn't any vacation." Max sighed long and hard. "So why did Jerry have you work your shift and mine? Wasn't Hector or anyone available?"

"There was a little scandal on Friday, when you left. Jerry found some weed in the back room and called up everyone to see whose it was or if anyone would point fingers, but no one did. No one's fessing up, and I'm the only one he can account for, so he pretty much fired everyone else."

"What?"

"Yeah, I think Mrs. Jerry might be holding out or something. He's been a prick lately."

Max ran a clawed hand through his hair. "Well, I'm here, so you can take off."

"I will in a second. Waiting for something to load here."

"How's the computer?" Max said. "I know exactly nothing about them."

"It's pretty decent. IBM, 16 megahertz, 4 megabytes of system RAM, Windows 3.1. Should make the day more interesting—or night." Tyler sat back and put his hands on his head. "That's right, I forgot, you hate computers, don't you?"

"Don't hate them, really," Max said. "I just get bad vibes from them, like one day it's going to start talking to me in a HAL voice. Try to destroy me."

"Well, we got just about a decade before that happens, right?"

"Why?"

"2001?"

"Oh, right."

Tyler crossed his legs. "Jerry's looking into hooking us up to the Internet, too."

"Oh right. Internet... God.... Hear the word floating around but still don't really know what exactly it is."

"It's a cyberspace-satellite thing, I think, where you can go to all these different places for companies or ads or school stuff."

"Okay. That doesn't really help."

"It's like electronic billboards, or the Yellow Pages. Jerry wants to put one up for the shop, actually."

"They'd allow that?"

Tyler shrugged. He clicked furiously but the screen had frozen.

"Hell with it," Tyler said. "I'm off."

The kid got up and Max assumed his seat.

"Oh, by the way," Tyler said as he gathered his things. "Some guy came in here earlier in the evening, like eight-ish, kind of a tall guy, scrubbed, yuppie-type. Asked about you."

"No name?"

"No name. Seemed disappointed you weren't here, though. When I said you were on a trip, he got kind of pale and asked if I knew who you went with. Told him I had no idea."

Max nodded.

"Okay, man, I'm gone."

"Yeah, go home and crash. Later."

"See you."

Nothing happened for the next three hours, a calm and empty night, and Max forced himself upon his sketchbook. *Draw, draw*. All efforts, all products of all efforts, came out plastic, unconvincing. *Come on, asshole*. Feldman... it was Feldman who'd siphoned, vampire-like, his drawing. Max had left his art in that unreal recess, buried in shadow, mere traces clinging to him, soon to dissolve in time. *Goddammit goddammit* goddammit!

A breath of relief when the door chimed open, and the night rushed in along with a purple-haired French girl in need of a vibrator — nice nice breasts, fun accent, brimming with desire tangible. When she left, the drawing got easier, sort of, a little more fluid, as if she'd delivered a short burst of life-energy upon which Max fed.

Vampire-like.

"I owe you, don't I?" Karen asked, as the van cruised down a vacant Centinela Avenue.

"Owe me what?" Dwayne said.

"Money... for everything."

"You already paid me."

"Yeah, but you and I both know that wasn't your full price. Plus, I owe you for the gas and for this trip."

Dwayne threw up an *eh, whatever* gesture but didn't refuse the offer.

"Just come on up," Karen said. "I'll cut you another check."

"Karen, honestly, don't worry about it—"

"Shush!" She clamped her hands over her ears. "I'm gonna give you more money! Final!"

Dwayne said nothing further as he slid the van into a tight space half a block from Karen's complex.

She opened the door and led Dwayne into darkness. A block north, Pico Boulevard spoke in hushed tones. Karen hurried to the kitchen light switch, then stopped by her room to unload her backpack.

Hands in pockets, Dwayne took in the scene before him: the coffee table a debauched skyline, towering bottles of vodka and gin and whisky; some dented beer cans, fallen on the floor; condom wrappers torn and strewn on the couch cushions. The odor of cigarettes and sharp skunky weed dominated the air.

"Someone had a hell of a time here," Dwayne said.

"Vivian's crazy like that," Karen said from her room. She came out with her checkbook in hand and went to the kitchen, where she poured herself a glass of water.

She fingered some paper on the counter.

"Looks like Viv actually wrote down my calls," she said. Her eyes widened. Under an exasperated breath, she uttered, "How'd he get *this* number?"

"Everything all right?"

She downed the rest of the water. "Were you planning on leaving soon?"

"You mean here? Or—"

"Los Angeles. Were you planning to leave Los Angeles soon?"

"Well, after your job I was. Had some stuff on the itinerary but it can wait if need be. Why? What's wrong?"

"I may need you to do something else for me, just to set my mind at ease. And if there is something going on, then maybe we can gather enough evidence to go to the cops."

Dwayne stepped forward. "What's going on?"

"Hold on a sec." She placed the checkbook and pen on the counter. "Be right back. Smallest bladder in the West, you know."

As she scurried off to the bathroom, Dwayne went over to the counter and picked up the slip of paper Vivian had left for her. The girl's handwriting was large and loopy, off-putting, but it was legible.

> *K—*
>
> *A James C. called like 50 times for Penelope...(?) He from ur work?*

III

Max slept for only four hours, the most he'd rested since returning from Twilight Falls a week and a half ago.

With sluggish momentum, he collected several pieces of art and took the Metro toward Venice Beach, carrying under his arm five works wrapped in a blanket—all the usuals, with one exception: *Moon Watch*. It sat now in his closet at his studio, the old acrylic face of Darren Higgins, the face that had become Clifford Feldman, sunk beneath three layers of Titanium White, the canvas now a virgin white soil in which anything could grow, entombing further the old work and the old face.

The sun shone high and lively and beating at the beach, but a constant breeze undermined its warmth. Portentous fog gathered out at sea, an encroaching marine layer like a ghostly cavalry waiting to charge.

Jiggling change. Dwayne's buddy. The bum. Johnny, was it?

"Support your local wino!" Johnny cried. "Help me to a liquor store! Help me forget my troubles!"

Max set up about twenty yards from Johnny on the fringe of a grassy hill, at the base of a lone drooping palm, an oasis in the grimy cement rivers walkways winding across the shoreline. *The sun's bright.* He fished through his pockets, checking for his sunglasses, then noticed something.

His neck was bare. The necklace... the gold cross... it wasn't there.

Oh God — what the — where is it — mattress — okay — took a shower — had it off — left it by the mattress — left it by the mattress — forgot it —

— forgot it.

Two young men, hands in a white-knuckle twine, stopped to survey his work.

"Oh, I like this one," one said, pointing to *Geometric Skull*.

"Little creepy, isn't it?" said the other with a higher voice. He pointed to *Angel Grass*. "What about that one? Might look good in your bathroom."

"How much for that one?" said the first.

Max cleared his throat. "That one's seventy-five."

"Hmm. Yeah, I could go with that one."

"This one?" Max made sure, gesturing toward *Angel Grass*.

They both nodded. Delicately, he handed it to the second man, who took it just as delicately. As the couple moved off with the piece, Max folded the money and stuffed it into his back pocket.

Then, just next to him: "Hey there." A familiar voice, muffled by the many others passing.

Max turned.

The guy from The Schoolhouse, the shop, the Mover and Shaker, clad now not in his money-clothes but in denim shorts and a collarless shirt. James — yes, this time he was sure of the name, but only because he'd now seen this man too often.

"Hey," said Max, with only fleeting eye contact. "How's it going?"

"Not too bad. Max, right?"

"Right."

"This looks like a good place to sell artwork. This where you make your sales?"

"For now. I've been in kind of a dry spell lately."

"I see. Well, I have some good news for you. I don't know if you remember, but I mentioned once to you a gallery that I was thinking of opening — "

"I remember, yeah."

"Well, it's a go. I've got the place, and I'm in

contact with a few artists, and I want to have the grand opening this summer."

"Really?"

"Indeed. I've even been working on a few pieces myself. I'm a bit of a sculptor. Well, *was* a sculptor. I'm kind of getting back into things. I haven't started them but I'm just formulating. I'm sure you know how that goes, getting things squared away."

"I know, yeah."

Get out of my goddamn face.

James nodded. "I wanted to let you know, too, that I really like your work. I saw some of it on the Internet, on the page for *Direct Canvas*."

"My stuff is on the Internet?"

"Uh-huh. There was one in particular I really liked. Can't remember the name of it, unfortunately, but when I saw it I felt The Spark. You know that—you feel it with women, you feel it with art. Just hits you. I want to do something like that."

While curious as to what piece he was referring, Max kept his replies to a minimum. "Glad to be of service."

Both men stared into the stream of people before them. The marine layer edged closer to shore and the air grew damp, breezes barbed with a chill.

James said, "I heard you were on a trip."

Max nodded. "Was up north, visiting family."

Visiting family hah visiting family what the what the—

"Traveling alone?" James said.

Finally Max faced him, made eye contact. "Why do you care?"

"No real reason. Just curious, that's all. Sorry to pry."

Wind snapping now, the cottony tendrils of fog curled lethargically inland.

"I guess I'll leave you be," James said. "I'm probably a nuisance unless I buy something, right?"

Max said nothing.

James Cannon walked the beach and thought of her.

She, a shimmering mirage in his mind that was growing stronger, riding every other synapse, becoming a stomachache in his brain. What would she say if he just... told her? If he upchucked these feelings and let her sort them out? She was probably used to guys doing that, but maybe from him she would find it distantly endearing, charming. He could be the exception. She was kinky, wild — she'd have to be to work at a place like The Schoolhouse, where just being an employee entailed risks. How much of a stretch was it to think she wouldn't take it one step further, give in to her curiosity by accepting at least a night with him?

"Penelope?" the girl on the other end had said, as if she were genuinely confused. "She's not available."

Twice now she hadn't been available. *Odd. Bad timing too, bad bad timing.* In her mourning, Teresa had not been given much to sex, and so much of his energy of late had gone into the office. Other things too... his art. *Yeah, what art? You wish.* Maybe Max could be his mentor. How degrading would that be? *Ask him. Ask him.* Max knew Penelope, too — somehow there had to be a way in. Yet all such ways seemed dark and narrow, perfect for the lesser creatures: the worms, the weasels.

She's avoiding me.

He wondered if her roommate had given her his messages. Hopefully, she wasn't creeped out by his calling. She was probably intrigued. It probably turned her on.

Maybe one day he could sculpt her.

Immortalize her.

Dwayne hated lawyers. Well-deserved reputation they had—every joke, corny or harsh, echoing some sad, animal truth. He hated investors too. There was a kinship between the two, the suits that thrived on base reflex, sharp-toothed instinct. This guy Cannon so conformed to the look, too—the clothes, the attaché case, the myopia of his movement, animated not on any one soul but an assemblage of souls sired from others. A Frankensoul.

"Can you keep an eye on this guy for me?" Karen had said in her apartment, just after they'd returned from the trip up north.

When he'd asked what was wrong, she bit her lip, her demeanor tightening. She sat tentatively on the edge of her couch, inches from her roommate's party mess, eyes lost in haunting possibilities.

"Nothing is wrong yet," she said. "This client of mine just creeps me out. I haven't worked, you know, where I work for very long, but I haven't had anyone as... serious as him."

"He's the guy who called fifty times?" Dwayne said.

"You saw the message," Karen said rhetorically. "Yeah. Seems a little crazy to me."

"To me too. What would you like me to do? See if he has a record?"

"I guess. I think maybe just the more I know about him the more at ease I'll be. Maybe."

She had dictated to him basic physical features and he had sketched his face. Then she'd given him the model and plates of his car.

"Sounds like you're more than creeped out," Dwayne said.

"I've learned to be on the defensive since leaving home." Karen had sighed. "I think I'm going to lie low. Rose'll be cool if I don't go in much this week. My appointment load is low. I won't take any more."

Preliminary searching had brought up no records, scarcely even a traffic violation. For several days now, Dwayne had watched him—long days at the office, a coffee run, even a Tuesday morning manicure. *Like I'm on safari,* he thought. First sighting had been at The Schoolhouse—yet with the way Cannon had walked in, briefcase in hand, it had seemed more business than pleasure.

Dwayne also saw him at the beach.

Max. He's talking to Max.

Once Cannon moved away, he approached Max, who sat on a blanket surrounded by his artwork, elbows rested on his knees—same position as when they'd met.

"Hey there," said Dwayne. "Back at the beach."

Max shook his head. "How many more people know I'm here?"

"Why were you chatting with that guy? You know him?"

"Not really. I've seen him at The Schoolhouse and at my shop. He's putting together an exhibit he wants me in."

"Exhibit?"

"Yeah, so he says."

"Karen tell you about him?"

"In a manner of speaking. I first saw him with Karen." Max hesitated. "Is... she okay?"

"She's all right, taking a few days off work."

"That guy, James," Max said, gesturing to the crowds. "He came into the Sirens Shop to buy Schoolhouse videos. He saw I worked there."

"He say anything?"

"Tried not to." Max was making sparse eye contact. "Like my mother liked to say, every bit of him spoke the truth except his mouth."

"What do you mean?"

"I don't know. He seemed on edge, antsy, too curious. Is—"

Max was interrupted by two older men in fisherman hats, collared shirts and swim trunks, who slowed to take in his work.

"Is this charcoal?" asked one of the men.

"It is."

"I'm gonna go," Dwayne said. "Take care of yourself, Maximo."

"You too." For the first time in their exchange, Max's eyes met his. They were stone. "Tell Karen to be careful."

Blink blink blink — the cursor patiently awaited input, the humming computer screen burning into his eyes, so infernally blank. Once again, Ritter surveyed his notes, twelve pages of crowded, serpentine text drawn from Feldman's exhibition, his interviews. There seemed little to say. In so many words, Bennett Wilson had even pridefully made the point that Neo-Naturalism encouraged very little discussion beyond the thing itself. It was the scooping out of wordless ideas — not ideas, maybe, but drives, raw emotions — and transmuting them into tangible visions.

Knowles wanted the coverage for the next issue. Ritter had time but the deadline was still tight because... writer's block. Every word had to be perfectly formed, perfectly placed, right out of the starting gate. Such a thing was impossible, of course. So why not take a cue from Feldman? Spew it all out, stream-of-consciousness, and sort it out as he progressed? But what was there to spew out? Ritter considered the dubious genius of Neo-Naturalism's influence on him: they championed something, and he recognized it, but couldn't find the words to describe it — a predicament seemingly at the heart of Feldman's philosophy.

"As we've made it!" said Feldman in his mind. "The words we've given ourselves, the methods we've given ourselves, have made such *Something* sadly ill-defined, walled it up behind glass. See but don't touch."

Touch... touch what? God? The ancient hermit living in some remote neural wilderness?

It didn't help that, with the forthcoming baby, Ritter's mind increasingly focused elsewhere. Angie was due in two weeks, but Dr. Fallon had said to be prepared in case labor happened sooner than expected.

No, not touch God. Be God. Assume the role people were born to play. To remember. To do what? To make breathing artworks?

Of course, writhing in this seething mess was the age-old question of what art was. To Ritter, art was everything made—artifice, after all. Anything could be art, so in a way he empathized with Feldman's thesis. Ritter certainly thought there were degrees of art, just as there were degrees of any profession or education—different grades, the minors and the majors. But what did *made* mean? People *made* bowel movements—were they art? No. And the very early art, Ritter considered, might have been as *blind* as bowel movements, generated less from an analytical frontal lobe than from the grander, infinitely patient intelligence that pervaded everything and held together bodies small and celestial alike.

Pure, clean expression.

Feldman, it seemed, wanted to go back to listening to that intelligence, but people didn't know if such intelligence truly existed. They knew their own mind, sort of. So the world, the cosmos, could not be considered art, an artifice, because the verdict was still out on whether or not it was indeed "made."

But if we're of this world, this cosmos, we're part of it, we are it, so why can't we just speak for it, which really means speaking as it, and proclaim our identity as it, the ultimate Maker, the ultimate Blind Maker that, through us, gave itself eyes to see and voice to shout its magnificence?

Ritter sighed. *I need a drink.*

Suddenly unnerved by the silence of his office, he turned on the desk radio—the weather, sports, an update on the King trial. The jury was still deliberating, and expected back soon. With a verdict.

MIKE ROBINSON

Chapter 7

I

Teresa's food had gone straight through him — those vegetables, all that fiber, crashing through and cleaning house. It was a good excuse to stay long in the john, a porcelain Fortress of Solitude in which to read his first issue of *Direct Canvas*, freshly arrived with a colorful expressionist piece on the cover attributed to a late, horn-haired Brooklyn artist, Jean-Michel Basquiat.

Yet an interior spread most interested James, an article on a Clifford Feldman, a former banker from Seattle who, now in his mid-fifties, had generated a bit of a rumble called Neo-Naturalism. What did that mean, exactly? This too had kept him on the fringe of the art scene: fibrous knowledge of its history and vicissitudes and all the key players therein. He knew the big names, of course, but mostly through cultural osmosis.

"Imagine," Feldman was quoted as saying. "In Cro-Magnon times, mode of artistic expression did not change for over twenty thousand years. There must have been something deeply, extraordinarily satisfying about such a mode and the reasons for it. It was a form of communion with nature and spirit. What higher value can one hold?"

Feldman strikes me as a belated mutant-child of romanticism, the author of the article, a Norman Ritter, had opined. Not a huge fan, James supposed.

I never like to classify my stuff, James thought.

Feldman seemed to be providing a permission slip for those like him. "It is a failed history," Feldman had also said. "Cram it all you like with masters and masterpieces. It is still a failed history."

One major impediment to James's own art, when one got beyond those more surface-level, such as Pops the Judge or the generally tame and tepid reception of his work, was the phantom responsibility James shouldered—and he imagined every American artist did, too—to create something New and Revolutionary.

Revolution: a word that strung together the DNA of the country. Something was not worth doing unless the artist could do it bigger, better, grander than anyone else, unless the artist pressed his name indelibly into textbooks, into journals, into popular consciousness. Yet at best, James's art was an occasional hobby. Compared with the more passionate among them—like the Max guy, from Sirens Shop—who thrived on it as sustenance, James was a watery wannabe.

And yet... maybe that was exactly the potential source of his own innovation. He could hug the wilder, untamed outskirts of expression, find something new that would flip mountains, leave a smoldering crater, persist on the tongues of succeeding generations, provide a lasting impact.

New and Revolutionary: wipe the slate clean, as Clifford Feldman intimated. Fuck the critics, the naysayers, the teachers, the parents. He was as much himself as he could be. The truth of people was as diverse as people themselves. Whatever nature had hidden away in his clay, even if she'd hidden it in only him, it was all true, it was all art, it was all, in a way, divine.

"Where do you get your inspiration?" they'd ask him. "What gets your juices flowing?"

He'd put an arm around Pene—no, Teresa. *Wait, fuck it. Come on, where is she? Not around. You're your own universe now. Make of it what you will.*

Penelope: the only person to have traipsed with him along those wild outskirts. She'd injected *him* back into him, reminded him how natural he could feel in his skin. She had said those things were okay. They didn't make him crazy. By comparison, what, then, were other aspects of himself with which he'd once wrestled, or resisted? James the Attorney? James the Artist? Those were basic no-brainer additions to the totem pole of his character. All beasts, all fragments, had within him a home. Because of her? Who could be sure, but she had helped.

James finished up, stood, and flushed the toilet.

Max awoke to a knock, not knowing how many it had taken to stir him. He dragged himself from the mattress and stumbled toward the door, tripping over an empty butcher tray.

Karen stood at his door. Her nervous disjointed energy struck him.

"What's the matter?" he asked.

"Just quit my job," she said, launching herself into the room.

Max shut the door. "Why? What happened?"

You know.

"James," she said. "It's that fucking James guy. You remember him?"

He nodded.

"He's...." Karen gave a hesitant chuckle, as if just understanding the world's punch line. "Okay, so he's buying The Schoolhouse. He's turning it into some kind of gallery."

"Art gallery?"

"Apparently."

Max shivered.

"I need a drink," Karen said. She riffled her pockets and brought out a clip of bills. "Where's the nearest bar?"

"I think there's one just a block and a half east of here, The Saloon."

"You all right joining?"

Max ran fingers through his hair. He was tired. Part of him never wanted to see or deal with Karen again. She brought with her a world too burdensome, too anarchic, too close to the bone.

"Sure," he said.

"Don't worry," she said as they made toward the door. "I don't need to lose my entire grip, just loosen a few fingers."

Decorated in the style of an old dude ranch, The Saloon was somewhere between a bar, a pub, and a museum. Karen ordered a Johnnie Walker Black on the rocks, Max ordered a beer, and they slid into a booth in the far corner, huddled beneath a large buffalo head.

Max tentatively lifted his beer and sipped it. It had been a decade since his last taste, but it wasn't as bad as he remembered.

"This is the longest I've seen you with your hair down," he said. "Not in a ponytail mood?"

"I think I left my scrunchie in Dwayne's van," Karen said. "Took it off when I napped, and just forgot about it."

"You could use a rubber band or something."

"They're rough on the hair, though. I figured I can let my hair breathe a little before I handcuff it again."

"Sounds like you're still in work mode."

Karen looked at him.

"Handcuffing... sounds like Schoolhouse lingo."

"Oh, right. Well, fetishes don't clock in and out."

Max took a longer, fuller sip.

"It's so weird. It just... ended. Dawn is such a sell-out."

"Who's Dawn?"

"The owner. She was so proud of the place, so proud to be... I don't know...."

"Providing scarce services?"

"I guess. That she up and sells it off to someone *whim-bam-boom* is just strange. He must have offered her a lot."

Max regarded her.

"You're not...." Karen began. "I mean, you said he talked to you about being a part of this new venture of his? This gallery?"

"He did. And no, there's no way I'm going to be a part of it."

Karen exhaled. "Truth be told, I'm not sure how you would be."

"What do you mean?"

"I don't know really anything about it, but I got an impression from Rose and Monica that he wanted them still there, that he wasn't going to lay them off."

"He gonna make it a half-gallery, half-S&M dungeon or something?"

Karen shook her head and drank more. "Who fucking knows."

Between two people, strangers not a week ago, how could so much accumulate so fast? A cosmic coercion, it seemed, playful strings of coincidence knotted in some impermeable truth or lesson, whatever it was. Suddenly he had a family. Even if Karen wasn't his true half-sister, she was family; they had shared enough in so little time. They'd held hands and descended to the cellar of their selves, explored corners never illumined — a lifetime's worth of closeness crammed into a mere weekend.

Relativity ever at work.

There were people like his co-worker Tyler, whom he'd known for years, yet about whom Max could probably not answer more than three basic questions. And yet, what did he really know about Karen other than what he felt about her? He could likely offer few facts about *her*, too, yet all intimacy with her was not fact-based but a nebulous intuition containing all things to know, and ready to portion out any answer when called.

"Do you think he was really drugging people?" Max asked abruptly.

Karen closed her eyes. "Maybe. Maybe they just wanted to be. We can't just do shit anymore. Everyone needs an excuse."

"You mean it was psychosomatic?"

"What does that mean?"

"Means you feel something but it's all in your mind."

"Oh, sure. I think so. When I was in high school in Baltimore, I went with some fraternity guys to a bar—"

"When you were in high school?"

"Uh-huh. I was seventeen. It's crazy easy for girls to get into bars there."

"Okay."

"Anyway, one of the guys went to get us drinks, and got these two other guys non-alcoholic beers without telling them. I think he wanted to get back at them for something—can't remember—but the guys got drunk anyway, all red-faced, busting up, acting stupid as hell. I'm surprised no one actually vomited. But they thought it so."

Max took this in and drank more beer.

To their left a figure appeared, a young man with gelled hair and a five o'clock shadow. Approaching them, his eyes trained laser-like on Karen. He leaned in toward her, ignoring and shutting out Max.

"Hey," he said. "What's up? I'm Dylan."

Karen glanced at him and made a revolted face. "Oh God, go clean your nose."

Dylan stiffened, cupped a hand over his mouth and nose, and scurried off toward the bathroom.

Karen grinned.

"I didn't see anything," Max said.

"Eh, there wasn't," she said. "But it's the quickest deflector." She sipped her whisky.

Max's gaze traveled about the gathering crowds, stopping at a brunette at the bar. She had striking blue eyes, little make-up but needing none of it, hair long and straight to her waist, and a tight figure in a blue dress from which long creamy legs protruded. She looked alone.

"She's hot," Karen said, steeliness in her eyes.
Max nodded.
"Go get her."
He snorted. "Right."
"Just try talking to her."
His head now swam from the beer. "I think I need another."
"Here." Karen held out her glass. "Take the rest of mine."

II

James spotted the van again, parked across the street, down 28th. Could it be one of Bendoni's cronies, waiting to pop him, bust his balls for the bombed trial? No, it was a clunker. And good God, it was a van, well below Bendoni, unless he'd farmed out work, or this was a cheap-o shot, assigned to one of the less professional hitters. James wasn't even worth a high-priced hit, apparently.

Stop and breathe. He closed his eyes, inhaled, exhaled.

But the van was real. He'd noticed it only two nights ago, on his way home from the office, a whale on wheels, wide baleen grill, body chipped and dented with travel—hippie-travel, dark tinted windows. He wondered why he'd even noticed it. Maybe because it stood out in a lot of BMWs and Mercedes. He imagined it abandoned there, full of explosives, imagined somewhere close an itchy finger poised and ready above a red button—the lot, the office, engulfed in radiating flames.

It had appeared again not far from the Baja Fresh where he sometimes ate lunch.

Then, outside Larry's place, from which James had stumbled tipsy after cards, he'd seen it again. Larry had known nothing about it, told him to go home, rest, and save his money for the next go-round, loser he was.

Loser.

There was no way I could have won that case.

Maybe James was supposed to notice him, given the conspicuousness of the vehicle. And who tailed people in a van anyway, anymore? The *unmarked van* was a Hollywood cliché. Seeing it, one might assume a bunch of wired-in FBI agents were having a pizza party, twisting all sorts of constitutional privacy laws.

Bullshit. I'm not a loser, not a pushover, not a guy to fuck with so Penelope watch this —

He went to the garage. From a box of old sports equipment, he drew an aluminum baseball bat, picking a long cobweb off the handle. He moved quietly from the side yard, and approached the vehicle from behind. No movement came from within, at least none that he could see.

His palms moistening, James went around to the driver's side, slightly hunched, and popped up in the window. *Any movement?* No. *Is there...?* Yes, someone was inside. He peered in to see the driver sleeping. *Sleeping!* Definitely not a hitter for the Family. He was wiry, bearded, wearing a ball cap and clothes that looked raided from a church donation box.

James tapped on the glass, and the man stirred, looked at him. James awaited the telling second, the moment of truth when the man's fearful eyes would betray panic, instantly legitimizing James's paranoia.

He's here for me.

In one full thrust, James sent the bat through the driver's side window.

The man's arms flew up and he yelped—*yelped who the hell yelps?*—as the glass blew across him, showering his lap, the dashboard, the floor.

"Who are you?" James said. "The fuck do you want?"

The man fumbled for something below his seat.

James raised the bat once more, strode forward... and met the hollow black mouth of a gun. The man's eyes burned. *Stalemated.* James's gaze slipped from the man's to the glass-stippled dashboard, where he spotted a girl's scrunchie. By the glow of the nearest streetlight, he could make out the velvety texture.

Penelope's. Is that hers? Hers?

James backed up a step. "You know her, don't you?"

With the gun still out, the man started the ignition but said nothing. With a herky-jerk of the steering wheel, he pulled out into the street and roared forward.

James sprinted after him and sent the bat directly into his left taillight, cracking it and spiraling chunks of plastic down the pavement. The van accelerated and James wanted to pursue, but stopped, breathing hard, and just glanced at the license plate: FRTNLV.

The hell is that?

He coughed, threw the bat on the lawn, and watched the van, now a block ahead. The vehicle's working taillight flashed a single red glare as the vehicle slowed to take a right turn. Then it was gone.

On one knock, Karen answered the door.

Dwayne took her firmly by the arm. "We need to get you out of here," he said.

Color drained from her complexion. "What?"

"James Cannon... he's dangerous. You need to get out of here for a while."

"Why? What happened?"

"Listen, he attacked my van, broke the driver's side window because he caught on to me. And a taillight."

"Why can't we call the cops on him?"

"I'd rather not deal with them," Dwayne said. "For one thing, my P.I. license is expired, and it'll be his word that I was following him and that busting my window was a pre-emptive self-defense thing. I also pulled the gun on him. But we should move fast. Better for now to just get you out and lay low. You quit your job anyway, right?"

"What about Max?"

"What about him?"

"Give me time to think," Karen said, "get my shit together and tell Max, see if he'll come with us."

III

Twenty minutes before the alarm, Max awoke. Close mournful wails, sirens, grew closer, exacerbating the battering ram behind both eyes. As the pain spread to his temples, he relaxed his jaw, realizing that he'd been gritting his teeth in his sleep.

He sat up, and aches scrambled needle-footed down his spine. He either had slept wrong or had been thrashed about by one hell of a dream.

Noises rose outside. Somewhere in the street, people were shouting, some voices worrisome, others weighted with imminent violence. A fire engine screamed in the distance, and glass shattered from hardly a block away.

Max went to the window and peered out, squinting against the glare of the sun. Initially, he saw nothing too out of the ordinary—two men hanging out on a brick storefront windowsill, picking at fast food wrappers; a kid running.

He looked southward.

Like some phantom addition to the skyline, a massive gray column of smoke rose through the buildings. First thought: a bomb had gone off. But there had been no explosion, none he'd heard. Max stared, mesmerized, caught in the stasis between revulsion and primal giddy awe.

More sirens erupted.

He tried to resurrect an old radio but found no new batteries. He didn't want to go outside. The roads appeared relatively calm, with only a handful of cars and people trickling across the pavement. It was all related, though: the aches, the sirens, the shouts, the smoke, the quiet. Something had happened. Something was wrong, wrong enough that perhaps his body had registered it in his sleep, tensing painfully in preparation for whatever unwanted thing stirred now in the gut of the city.

His phone rang, and he went to get it.

"Maximo."

"Yeah."

"You okay?"

"I'm okay. What's happened?"

"People are rioting because of the Rodney King trial. Cops got set free."

Max wasn't sure how to react.

Dwayne continued, "Most of the rioting is in South Central, but they say there's some shit going down in your neck of the woods, too. Karen and I are coming over to get you."

Because I'm the helpless person in grave danger. Thanks. But he couldn't argue. He was. And who else did he know who had a car? They were his ticket out of here.

"Okay," he said.

"On the way."

He hung up, and then suddenly a crash sounded down below, followed by a scream — a woman's. He listened to the commotion rolling and banging on the ground floor, echoing up the building. More glass shattered as voices grew louder, layered, thundering the walls.

Max went to the door, checked the peephole, and saw his neighbor Renaldo standing in the hallway peering down over the railing. Slowly, he pulled the door open and emerged beside him.

"Que paso?" said Renaldo. "Esta loco!"

Max said nothing.

"Tengo miedo. Oh, Dios—"

Down in the lobby moved three men in oversized clothes and ball caps. Two of them wielded metal baseball bats. There was a third, too, barely visible from where he stood but certainly the most animated.

The man stood just outside, flailing above something — a human form, a person lying prostrate, rumpled and bloodied on the sidewalk beneath a barrage of strikes from the third man's bat.

Beating him. Jesus. Max knew the victim: Gonzo. *Jesus he's beating him beating him to death —*

Max scurried back into his room and shut the door. More clanging came, then more police sirens; close, then distant; distant, then close. He was drained of all else, reduced to some white yellowy adrenal core, a tattered rough-sketch of a person. Frantically, he searched for the gold cross but found it nowhere. How could it have disappeared like that?

Voices of the thugs drew closer, pounding about, ascending the stairs. Outside, the hiccupping roar of a helicopter flew southbound, and others flew farther away, some media, probably — gnats, flies, celebrating a death-stench.

Max huddled on his mattress, stared at his pieces, the Wall, the sketchbooks.

More banging, now closer, and harsh rapping, the force of twenty concussions delivered on his neighbors' walls and doors. Shouts Rose in Spanish and broken English, as a baby cried and a kid cried.

Another bang, splintered wood, and then came a scream — Ms. Feliz, Max surmised. She'd told him she was a retired grade-school teacher What they were doing... what they were doing to her....

Stop it make it go away stop please fucking stop —

Yelling this time, as his neighbor James Randolph cussed, warned of police, of private firearms. After a pattering of feet came *clang*, *thud*, and the *rap-a-rap-bang-bang* of metal bats dragged across the railing bars. The sudden apocalyptic crash of a gunshot rang out.

Oh God I'm going to die. Get out of my house God get out of my fucking house! *God is here with us. Dearest Lord, we pray.*

Demons. Devils. Screaming. You *shot* him. Don't shoot. *Jesus*! Get out. The panicked pace of multiple feet. His wall rattling against the ruckus.

Max ran to the window and surveyed the fire escape. *So high up.*

Another shout came behind him, outside his studio. *Get out now.* Christ get out *now*.

Glass shattered and there came a roaring rushing sound, heated and elemental, and Max knew, at some intuitive level, the scourge now unleashed just outside his door.

He hurried onto the fire escape, which swayed and squealed. The streets swooned beneath him as fine particles of ash sprinkled over the city. Several miles away, the pillar of smoke had grown thicker, darker.

He reached the ground, but the relief did not last. He was vulnerable again, dropped from his little cabin into the hard, choppy sea.

Dwayne's coming.

He made his way to the other side of the street, and turned back. Smoke curled from his apartment building, from its pores, spreading, gathering. People on lower levels spilled from the main entrance. Others climbed onto the fire escape as he had. He watched in particular the smoke, like effluvial eyelashes on the dark-eyed windows, the hints of blazing color beyond. *My window too?* Yes, his. That was his window, where he'd just come from—*God, oh God*—snorting and coughing flames.

The sidewalk now pulsed with people. Fire trucks wailed closer and closer.

He waited. Shuddering, terrified, powered by an energy larger than he, Max waited.

"There's definitely shit happening downtown," Dwayne said, repeating the radio newsman's words as if Karen weren't two feet away.

She didn't say anything, only fidgeted and rubbed her clammy hands together.

You're leaving, she thought. *You're leaving again. Smoked out.*

For a short while, they hurtled down the I-10 freeway, until running into a slowdown just past West Los Angeles.

"You know where you're going, right?" she asked.

Dwayne nodded. "Think I do."

She looked at him. Wind from the broken, unfixed driver's side window lashed at his hair and clothes. Her window was open to catch the smoke.

"Don't worry, I do," he said more assuredly.

"Hundreds of people are taking to the streets," came the low drone of the radio. "The presence of law enforcement is having minimal to no effect on the crowds.... We're looking here at the intersection of Normandie and Florence, where a truck driver has just been pulled from his truck. It appears he's being attacked... oh God... this is awful just *awful*.... Should things grow worse, Mayor Bradley might declare a State of Emergency...."

Karen reached over and turned it off.

In twenty, three-hour minutes, they reached Max's building, now surrounded by fire engines and police cars. Twice they circled the block, navigating the flashing lights, the people, the remnant smoke from the fading fire that had left its charred teeth marks all over the complex.

"Holy shit," Dwayne said. "That's his building."

Karen breathed, hard. They drove, and drove.

"There he is," she said, pointing.

They spotted one another at the same time. Max huddled by a payphone, secluded at the mouth of a small alley one block from the burning site.

Once, Max had heard there were eleven dimensions composing the universe, existing astride one another, sometimes overlapping, intersecting, a playful orgy of worlds. And, as with any such congress, there sometimes emerged what were called "baby universes," cosmic fetal-bubbles that, while bearing markers of the parent worlds, nonetheless individuated to grow and develop however they might.

Max possessed little mental agency for physics, but these theories, tattered as they were in his memory and his understanding, comforted him now, because inside Dwayne's van he was encased in a new baby universe, a universe arisen from the inexplicable chaos of the older, more domineering one, an embryonic glimpse of new realms. This new universe-on-wheels did not provide answers, but at least it asked them; at least it was a world of searching and of possibilities.

"Glad we could get to you in time, Maximo," Dwayne said quietly, as if embarrassed to inject words into a situation currently so defiant of comprehension.

Max sat quietly as the van climbed the on-ramp to the I-10 freeway and chugged and sped, sped and chugged.

"We're leaving," Karen said.

Max leaned forward. "What?"

"We're leaving town," Dwayne said. "Actually, not because of what's happening now. We want to get *her* out—" Dwayne thumbed toward Karen. "—until things cool down."

Questions rose in Max's throat but were cut off by the sudden realization of what, *who*, they were talking about.

"James," he said. "It's James, isn't it?"

Silent, prickly acknowledgment.

"What's he done?" said Max. "What's he done to you?"

"It's okay," Karen said. "He didn't do anything, not to me, not yet, but... I'm taking precautions, you could say."

Max glimpsed in her short pause an unspoken transgression. He looked back and forth between her and Dwayne. "What happened?"

"You wonder why I can't roll up my window?" Dwayne said. "Because it isn't there. Crazy fucker caught on to me and smashed my window."

Max put his face in his hands and rubbed his brow. "Oh man." He rubbed his eyes, which stung. "Can't we go to the cops?"

"It would be too complicated," Dwayne said with unexpected finality.

"I'm only twenty," Karen muttered. "Already running again."

Max began, "Would you have even told me about this, if, y'know...?"

"There hadn't been the riots?"

"Yeah. I mean—"

"Max," Karen said in her shut-up tone. "Of course we would have."

He sat back, his simmering body cooling once more, thoughts emerging from hidden places like survivors after a raging storm. Within him broiled a bedraggled and wrecked place, but still upholding, still him, body and mind and soul intact, though now hollowed out as somewhere, miles back, his remaining pieces, those baby universes sprung from him, now shriveled and blackened, ablaze in their ashen return to the elements.

Don't think about that. There are others elsewhere in the world, hung in galleries, on people's walls, in bathrooms. The tiny copies in your wallet.

"Where are we going?" Max said.

"Not exactly sure yet," Dwayne said. "I was thinking we'd just drive for now. But we could stop in Barstow to get our bearings, figure out some kind of plan, maybe."

Karen's eyes closed.

Max stared hazy-eyed out the windshield at the traffic bobbing and blinking around them, at miles and miles of cement and sky, and red brake-light glares against the gloom. The freeway led to the highway, the city gradated toward the vast hard-kneaded country, through stipples of civilization until there was nothing but raw rumpled plains, wide and forever.

She isn't here.
Where the hell is she?

James gripped the steering wheel tighter. His brain raced. She hadn't been to The Schoolhouse in days. She had missed his meeting.

Gone, she's gone, avoiding you, wants nothing to do with you. Can't you see what's wrong with you what's wrong with you —?

He kept at least three cars between him and them on the eastbound I-10 freeway, which then turned into the I-15 toward Barstow. *Good solid buffer. They won't notice.* He imagined heads were swimming with the riots, too. What bullshit that was, but maybe helpful, at least to him — a good distraction.

She knows she knows she knows she sees you.

No, he was okay, especially since he now drove Teresa's car, and not his own.

IV

By nightfall, the gas needle trembled just above empty, yet they rolled on, speeding across the desert beneath the wide dome of the sky, the wispy clouds like squiggly snow-tire tracks tracing away toward the horizon. Within fifty miles of Barstow, muscled clouds appeared, bunched up in a grand conspiracy of storm. The gray sheet of rain ahead veiled the spread of homes and buildings on an otherwise desolate landscape. As they moved into it, raindrops pop-thudded loud and harsh on the van.

"How about we find a motel for now?" Dwayne said. "Before we head any farther. We can decompress a little, rest, figure out what to do."

In silence, Max and Karen agreed.

They entered Barstow, its pebbled streets amphibious with rain-slick, thunder a cosmic throat-clearing, the horizon aflutter in lightning. In desert country there was a divine rawness to the weather, which dominated all here.

They found a Motel 6, its vacancy sign sputtering. Karen and Dwayne dashed into the lobby while Max waited in the back seat. Thousands of nails drummed the roof of the van, as if the rain were trying to coax out of this mistaken instrument some kind of maddening rhythm.

They were given Room 5.

"We're just staying here one night," Max said, sitting on the edge of the bed. "Right?"

"That's the plan," said Dwayne. He thumbed toward the street. "I'm going to grab some gas. We can leave first thing tomorrow. I may hit the store, too. You want me to pick up anything, food-wise?"

"I think I'm okay," Max said.

Karen checked her cigarette supply and shook her head.

Dwayne looked at them both, then sprinted back to the van, rummaged a bit, and returned with a dirty towel. Karen and Max leaned forward as he unraveled it, revealing, like some parent might a hideous babe, his single-action revolver.

"Keep this with you, in case," he said.

Blank stares.

"As a precaution," he said. "I noticed a car behind us for a long way. It's a highway, so everyone's traveling far, but this guy was with us since we left Los Angeles. At least that's when I noticed him. Didn't get a good look, though."

"Jesus," Karen said, taking the towel and gun. "Okay."

Thunder grumbled and, as if in rebuke, the rain strengthened. Dwayne flipped up his collar, shoved his hands into his pockets, and hurried through the silvery-wet column back toward the van.

Karen shut the door and slid the bolt, then dumped the gun on the nightstand and backed away from it.

"I hate guns," she said. "I can handle whips and chains, paddles and knives, but guns...."

Max sat still. "He'll be back soon," he said. "Soon."

James wasn't entirely sure if they were on to him. They'd given no indication, but what indications could they have given? Of course, if that grubby driver was any sort of actual investigator, he would have all his sensory dials turned up. But, clearly, the guy wasn't that good. He was sloppy, cheap. It was probably why Penelope had used him—good rate—but one got what one paid for.

A broken window. Cocksucker.

Cunt.

For many miles, he kept multiple car lengths between them. As they turned off in Barstow, he continued driving, taking a later exit, then turned back and cruised the streets. Either they were pulling off to stay the night, or they were swinging by for a quick bite—fast food or a grocery store or a motel. There wasn't much else, to be honest. Regionally, Los Angeles was like a brilliant sun in an empty and loser solar system.

Besides, that van, like something out of some '69-hearted Boomer's wet dream, was easy to watch.

The Motel 6.

He parked half a block away, and watched. The grubby driver was leaving, and James now knew the room.

Okay. The best way to approach this... what's the best way to approach her?

She was with the grubby driver and that guy Max from the sex shop. There was no way to do this without pissing on his image, at least with her. *Followed me all this way?* He was over the edge now, a crazy fucking stalker. But how callous was she? It was all theater, lying to him. All this time, he felt like she'd been building him toward something, like he himself had been building toward something, but which he'd been denied suddenly, whatever it was. An answer. A release.

A knock came on the door, muffled by the storm and the television, which Max muted.

Another.

They shared a glance. Dwayne? No. He'd just left, and he had a key, unless he'd forgotten it.

Then, through the watery patter, "Penelope?"

Max's gut tingled, and Karen turned white.

"No," Karen hissed. "No no what the *fuck*—"

Max sprang to the edge of the bed, huddled close by the nightstand where lay the toweled gun.

Karen stood between him and the door, frozen.

"Penelope," the stalker said. "Whatever your name really is... come on, please... I just want to talk to you. I know you're there."

You're going to use the gun, Max thought. *You're going to have to use the fucking gun.*

A gray shadow appeared in the window, blurred by the curtain. Through a small, parted interstice, an eye appeared, crisp and blue—staring, curious, determined.

The rain beyond pattered and crackled.

The shadow raised a fist and rapped on the glass. "Penelope? It's raining out here. I know this is weird, but can't I come in?"

"I'm calling the police," Max said. He hovered his hand over the phone. *Why await Karen's approval? Just call. Just call!* He watched as she crept closer and leaned in to the peephole.

She turned to him. "I think I can talk him down."

"What? Ka—"

With the security chain still in place, she carefully opened the door. The cacophony of the storm grew two-fold, tearing and smattering. Still an energetic shadow, the man moved fast into the sliver of gray light.

Terror struck Max that he might look in and see him by the bed, so Max left the phone and hurried over behind the television.

You left the gun. Goddammit.

"Penelope?"

"Mr. Cannon," Karen said, speaking to him through the thin opening—no Southern accent, Penelope dead and buried. "What are you doing?"

Barely audible in the storm, he said, "I want to talk to you. You just up and disappeared."

"I quit." She lowered her head. "Please leave me alone. I have the police on hold."

"The phone's right there," he said, pointing inside. "It's on the hook."

There was some flirty delight in the man's patronizing tone, as if he were convinced she was still playing "Penelope" with him.

Max stepped closer.

"Why did you quit?" James said. "Aren't favorite clients entitled to a little notice? What's your real name?"

"That's all personal," she said. "Please leave me alone, or I will call the police."

She went to close the door, but James reflexively clutched it, resisting.

He's not gonna leave. You son of a bitch. Max thought nothing else. A great upswell of rage took him, dark noisome contents plunged loose. An ancient, barbaric intelligence took hold of his mind and matter.

He ran at the door. Karen had little time to process but moved deftly against the wall as Max, hands outstretched, put his whole weight into shutting the door. A wooden thunder roared, followed immediately by the crackle-*pop* of bone and a shrill scream, James's fingers crushed and quivering in the doorjamb.

"Fuck oh *Jesus* fuck *me*! *Fuck me*!"

Karen gasped. "Holy shit, Max!"

Max threw her a wild furtive glance, then slid open the security chain and thrust open the door.

Karen maneuvered out of the way.

The rain crashed hard, so hard, as James stumbled back on the walkway, knees bent, right hand twisted and bloody, torn. Tears streamed down his face. He looked pale. Maybe he would faint.

Max went to him, landed a blow across his face, and blood dotted the cement. *Fuck that hurt.* Teeth scraped his skin, the harsh impact vibrating up his forearm, yet the pain blended fast with the escalating adrenaline.

"Get out of here!" Max screamed. "Get the fuck *out* and get *out of my house*!"

"Jesus Max!" Karen said, light-years behind him. "Max!"

He took James by the collar and rammed him against the wall—little to no resistance, still crying. Max slammed him a few times more, James's head once striking the stucco.

Yes that's it bash his skull in. Open his brains right here, let the rain clear 'em out. Nature you fucked this one up. Take it back. Take it all back. Try again.

"Max!"

He thrust James back to the walkway, where the man teetered on tenuous feet before collapsing to his knees, the rest of him supported by his single good hand, the other raised and bent and dangling like dead wind chimes.

Max hurried back into the room.

Terribly white, Karen was at the phone, receiver to ear. "I'm calling 9-1-1."

She's looking at you like she looked at him. Good.
No. Shut up. Calm down.

A figure rose again in the window. A shadow. *Him.*

"Motherfucker!" James shrieked. "Get back out here! Let me in! Fucker! Fucking cowardly *fucker*!"

A loud thud banged out, like a bird striking glass, then a crack and limbs flailing. In his movements behind the curtain, James became amorphous, a bulky man-thing, a faceless monster siphoned from childhood nightmares.

"He's breaking the window," Max said in barely a whisper.

"He's coming in," Karen rasped into the phone. "He's breaking in!"

One more strike and the window broke, shattered into translucent fangs knocked about on the floor. In whistled wind and cold.

"Motherfuckers!" James screamed. "Fucking pussy faggot!"

Suddenly there was a leaden *thud*, and the shadow fell, melted below the windowsill.

Another now stood in its place, and through the whispering hole in the glass, Max heard the voice. "Now we're even for my window."

V

He hadn't drunk coffee in three years, but today gave himself a free pass. Newborn Michael had kept him and Angelica up pretty much all night. Ritter was doped up on the red-eye hour. In this state, every surface looked inviting for sleep.

Dazed, with a black coffee in hand and a folded *Los Angeles Times* tucked under his arm, Ritter rode the elevator up to Ramon Plaza's third floor, home of *Direct Canvas's* fancy new — well, year-old — suite. Long slow day today, but he had a kid, a new purpose and a new dimension to his life and to everything. He was a father. How was that possible?

He occupied himself with the mail stack — more letters about Feldman, about Neo-Naturalism; children's drawings, mostly, from eager *my-kid-is-a-genius* parents, from *you're-going-to-be-the-star-I-never-was* parents. Now a parent himself, he thought he understood slightly better the source of this delusion. He'd probably understand even better as Michael grew, yet still he resented it, resented Feldman for encouraging it.

After all, the arts were already the target of snickers from the likes of the sciences. "Anyone can do that," some of the more arrogant might say, "not like brain surgery or aeronautics." Sure, anyone could do *this*, but try being Rembrandt. Try summoning Tolstoy to your pen. Can't learn that. One could learn the numbers and puzzles of brains and rockets, but one couldn't learn sublimity, couldn't snatch that spark in a bottle and label it and quantify it. Of course, according to Feldman, sublimity lurked in everyone.

Other mail came from bus drivers, addicts, janitors, policemen, clerks — all kinds of people, all kinds of art. *I sneezed on the sneeze guard at a Sizzler salad bar*, one woman wrote, with an accompanying picture, *and if you'll notice, it's the constellation Orion! I don't follow much astrology but the stars could be telling me something...?* Or the decidedly viler submission of a dark red sheet covered with Pollock-like streaks of dried semen. *I call it* The Orphaned, the man had written.

Soon Ritter turned to his *Los Angeles Times*.

Only a week ago, the anarchy in southeast and downtown L.A. had subsided. What a time to bring a kid into the world. Bad omens. The worst civil disturbance in United States history, they'd called it. Virtually every hour, images of the chaos had monopolized the airwaves.

The main section of the newspaper offered full of coverage of the riots—the beginnings, the hellish middle, the aftermath. They offered scattered uplifting stories about what various communities and organizations were doing to help the affected areas. The pages were checkered with pictures taken by freelance and staff photographers. So much energy and movement captured there. So much rage. Sadness. Figures running. Fires. Bloodied faces. Destroyed storefronts. Smoke billowing. Something out of an apocalyptic science fiction film. Terrible to say, but it was.

One blurb noted an African-American photographer named Gregory Wesley, whose work was featured in the pages. Next month, Bergamot Station would set up a small exhibition of his riot-born images, which Ritter admired: stark contrast, dynamic angles, poignant and provocative, taking a bite from reality. Art risen from tragedy, a colorful bud sprouting up through a skull's eye, art the ultimate healer, diagnostic tool, and prophet — if folks paid more attention.

Somewhere in the middle of all the coverage, between the articles and photographs and editorials, a full page of thumbnail pictures depicted various faces, their names and ages captioned under each one.

Toward the top of the section a single word stood out:

Missing

It listed those lost, those who'd slipped through the dark ruptures. There had to be more, many more, in fact, than were shown — too many younger faces, children and teenagers. Many were minorities, Latino and African-American the most represented, some Korean.

Ritter noticed one face — *recognized* one face — and his breath stalled.

Max Higgins, 28

VI

Max walked from the convenience store, munching on a Snickers bar, the Arizona heat unbearably thick, like being wedged in a dry armpit. He supposed it was better than Florida, which he'd heard was rather like being squeezed in a wet armpit.

How about just staying out of the armpits?

He slid the change into his wallet. As he was about to return it to his pocket, a thought struck him. He reopened the wallet, unfurled the accordion string of card-sized prints of all his work, then took one out—*Angel Grass*—went to the nearest parked car, and slipped it under the windshield.

Karen emerged from the store and saw him. "What are you doing?" She watched him as they returned in tandem to the van.

Max shrugged. "Sprinkling breadcrumbs?"

He dropped two more toward eastern Arizona, another not far beyond the New Mexico border—a belt of his work across America. He liked that; drops of him over the landscape.

Come Georgia, he'd left behind all but one.

He looked at it. Where to leave it the last bit of the parent universe, saying goodbye, baby universe awaiting, forged in the heat of multiple forces, the fruit of him and of fate. All those—what was it?—all those creators, destroyers, collectors, and teachers conferring, tinkering, ever-crafting, ever-creating—tearing down, compiling, building, spreading the word.

Spreading the word.

He turned the last card over and wrote on the back. A day later, he slipped it into the mail.

> *Mr. Ritter,*
> *Teach them well about me.*
> *Or not.*
> [Dot-dot-curve. Smiley face.]

The van trundled on through the shimmering Georgian hills, a bright and vivid fairy-tale green, pregnant rolling pastures. Max stared at it all, and turned to his sketchbook, new and blank, recently purchased in Oklahoma. He managed some loose doodles and lines, and nothing else.

"Still nothing coming, Maximo?"

He met Dwayne's eyes in the rearview mirror. "Not yet."

"You'll come upon something. Just a dry spell."

They sped ahead, farther, and the sun edged cautiously down toward the hills, lending highlight to their already beautiful melodrama.

In the passenger seat, Karen stirred from a nap. "Where are we?"

"Almost to Atlanta," Dwayne said.

"We can go wherever," Karen said. "I'm really not in any rush to go back to Baltimore."

"You don't have to," Max said. "At all."

"I know," Karen said, picking at her fingernails. "But it's... *me* there. I can't just drop it totally. I feel like I split myself in two, and that I need both versions of myself. Where you come from... you forget that. You forget it all. I don't know."

"Can't get to high school without grade school," Dwayne said.

"What?"

"Never mind." Again, Dwayne looked in the rearview mirror. "Hey, Max?"

"Yeah?"

"Can you get me a cola? Out of the cooler back there?"

"Sure."

Max crawled over the backseat bench, tossed aside loose papers and a blanket, and opened the cooler. Sitting inside next to a can of sliced peaches was the vial Karen had stolen from Feldman.

He stopped, picked it up, jostled it, popped off the cap, and sipped.

Salty, for sure.

"Everything okay, Maximo?"

His answer delayed: "Yeah, fine."

"Cool. Then what's taking so long with that soda?"

Max grabbed the can, and one for himself, then shut the cooler.

THE END

MIKE ROBINSON

About the Author

A writer since age six and a professional one since nineteen, Mike Robinson has published nine novels and over twenty pieces of short fiction. In addition to the "Twilight Falls" series, he is the author of *The Prince of Earth*; *Skunk Ape Semester*; *The Atheist*; *Dreamshores: Monster Island*; *Dishonor Thy Father* (with M.J. Richards), and *Too Much Dark Matter, Too Little Gray: A Collection of Weird Fiction*.

A native of Los Angeles, he is also an independent producer and screenwriter, with a feature supernatural thriller debuting in 2021. In between, he is a literary editor, hiker, swimmer, traveler, and amateur human.

For more, please visit Mike online at:
Website: www.Mike-RobinsonAuthor.com
Goodreads: Mike Robinson
Twitter: @MikeSkunkApe
Facebook: Mike Robinson Author

What's Next?

Book 3 in the "Enigma of Twilight Falls" series, *Waking Gods*, is set to release in late spring or early summer of 2020.

WAKING GODS

Meet Adrian Foster, a young and reclusive Los Angeles man with an extraordinary gift that has informally brought him the nickname "The Human Master Key." When a new victim of a vicious serial killer turns up in the woods by Twilight Falls, California, Adrian reunites with eccentric detective Derek Adams in probing the occult lore surrounding the town—the town in which Adrian was born and raised, the town in which he left behind many a ghost, the town whose dark central spirit will force him on a harrowing journey through the rugged bottomlands of another's psyche... as well as his own.

More from Evolved Publishing

We offer great books across multiple genres, featuring high-quality editing (which we believe is second-to-none) and fantastic covers.

As a hybrid small press, your support as loyal readers is so important to us, and we have strived, with tireless dedication and sheer determination, to deliver on the promise of our motto:
QUALITY IS PRIORITY #1!

Please check out all of our great books, which you can find at this link:
www.EvolvedPub.com/Catalog/

Thank you!